BRICKMAKERS

Also by Selva Almada and available in English

Dead Girls
The Wind That Lays Waste

BRICKMAKERS

A Novel

Selva Almada

Translated from the Spanish by Annie McDermott

Graywolf Press

This publication is made possible, in part, by the voters of Minnesota through
a Minnesota State Arts Board Operating Support grant, thanks to a legisla-
tive appropriation from the arts and cultural heritage fund. Significant support has also been provided by Target Foundation, the McKnight Foundation,
the Lannan Foundation, the Amazon Literary Partnership, and other generous
contributions from foundations, corporations, and individuals. To these organi-
zations and individuals we offer our heartfelt thanks.

MINNESOTA
STATE ARTS BOARD

**CLEAN
WATER
LAND &
LEGACY**
AMENDMENT

Brickmakers is published within the framework of "Sur" Translation Support
Program of the Ministry of Foreign Affairs, International Trade and Worship of
the Argentine Republic. Obra editada en el marco del Programa "Sur" de Apoyo a
las Traducciones del Ministerio de Relaciones Exteriores y Culto de la República
Argentina.

Published by Graywolf Press
250 Third Avenue North, Suite 600
Minneapolis, Minnesota 55401

www.graywolfpress.org

Published in the United States of America

ISBN 978-1-64445-069-7

2 4 6 8 9 7 5 3 1
First Graywolf Printing, 2021

Library of Congress Control Number: 2020951433

Cover design: Carlos Esparza
Cover art: Carle Vernet, *Wild Horses Fighting*, c. 1820. Art Institute of Chicago.

For Lolo Bertone, brickmaker,
beautiful free spirit

BRICKMAKERS

The Ferris wheel has emptied out, but the seats are still swaying gently. Must be the dawn breeze.

To Pájaro Tamai, sprawled on his back, it's like the giant wheel is still turning. But it can't be, because there's no music. He can't hear a thing: his head is full of white noise. White like the sky—he's never seen it this way—with the ride partly silhouetted against it, a blurry smear of machinery, which is all his eyes can take in.

He squints in case that stops the spinning. It makes it worse: he feels dizzy and now it's not just the Ferris wheel moving but the whole world.

He feels dizzy, just like when he was still on the ride. He and Cardozo had climbed into the double seat with a just-opened beer, the bottle spewing out thick white foam. Before pulling down the iron safety bar, the guy working the ride tried to confiscate the beer and they just laughed in his face. The guy shrugged and didn't insist. He'd had to say something because of fairground regulations, but if these piece-of-shit indios wanted to get themselves killed, that was fine by him.

The first time around went in fits and starts, a slow climb as the rest of the seats were filled. When they reached the top, Cardozo began spitting on the people below, who squinted up at him and cursed. Pajarito laughed and took a slug of beer and looked out over the town: the lights, dense along the streets in the center, thinned toward the outskirts; over La Cruceña, his neighborhood, there was only a handful.

Then the wheel picked up speed and they were spinning like crazy. They let out high-pitched sapucai shrieks and went on swigging from the bottle. Cardozo whooped and shook his head like a wet dog. The third time around he unzipped his fly and started pissing, waving his dick from side to side and splattering the riders below. Pájaro's ribs ached from laughing so hard. He felt high, happy and powerful.

Now, down here, his head buzzing and the sky so white it hurts. Pure blinding light like in the sci-fi movies when they took the little ones to matinees at the Cervantes. He's tired. Too much partying, he thinks. You play, you pay. He wants to shut his eyes in case that helps with the dizziness. He starts letting his eyelids drop, and then suddenly he gets it and opens them as wide as they'll go, making a superhuman effort to keep them that way because it's hit him and he realizes he's dying.

Pure rotten air filling his nostrils. Marciano Miranda is sprawled on his stomach, with one eye open. Face flat in the swampy puddle the ground has become after days of the fair. The grass burned away by footsteps, piss trails, vomit. It's always like this when there's a fair or a circus. A circus is worse: After they take down the cages, the weeds are black all the way to their roots from the animals' hot, heavy bodies. It takes months for the local wasteland to recover, and just as it starts to look nice again, another lot set up their stalls. Not that anyone cares. When it's empty, the only people who use it are couples needing a place to fuck. The real fun is when it gets busy, when it fills up with colorful lights and music and folks from out of town.

If Marciano is thinking about this right now, it's only because he's up to his eyeballs in the foul-smelling muck.

He raises one eye, trying to glimpse something beyond the dark stains on the ground. But the eye tires and sinks back to the layer of moldy leaves.

And here I am in white pants, he thinks.

"You look like a stud from a telenovela," Angelito had said as he was getting ready at home before hitting the town. Brand-new, spotless, tight, outlining his manhood, shirt tucked in all the way around.

Marciano looked at himself in the wardrobe mirror and saw his brother Angelito on the bed behind him, stretched out in his underwear like a rent boy, fanning himself with a magazine. He had an urge to spin around and bring the belt in his hand down hard on the boy's back, but he stopped himself. He didn't want a big fight with his mom before going out, it would ruin his night.

Soon he'd pull the plug on Ángel's ways. Maybe even that night, if he got lucky. Dead dogs don't bite, after all, and he knew it was Pájaro Tamai who'd gotten his teeth into his brother. Then a clean slate, a new start. Force the kid to eat pussy all day long, if that's what it took, till he got over his obsession with sucking dick.

But in the mirror he still threatened to smack him. Goddamn nerve, talking like that. He was the oldest, he deserved respect. He couldn't let this cocksucker carry on like they were with a bunch of fags.

Now none of that seems to matter. Lying here in the mud, he's tired and cold. Must be the dawn dew.

"Where the hell is Pajarito?!"

Their father's booming voice on waking up paralyzed the little Tamais, who ranged from two to seven years old. Whenever he got up to check the kids' room, one was always missing: Pajarito, six, the second child but the eldest boy, and the only one to break their father's ban on going out during the siesta.

Tamai was a harsh man and he didn't hold back when it came to enforcing his will. The siblings' loyalty was weak and another shout was enough to make it crumble. Even the initial silence, which could have been taken for complicity with the runaway, was just bewilderment from the mugginess and heat. They weren't going to stick their neck out for the rebel; after all, while he was off having a blast, they were floating in the fetid limbo of their room.

"He's gone to the canal"—and they'd point at the window through which Pajarito had taken flight once their dad was down for the count.

Tamai would pull on his trousers and shirt, grab the bicycle and the leather rebenque, and set off in pursuit. Most of the time, on reaching the canal, he found all the local kids jumping into the filthy water or dangling fishing lines—all except for his son. Pajarito was already away through the fields, tipped off by his inner alarm clock that his father was beginning to stir. Every so often Tamai got there first and landed a couple of lashes right on the boy's bare, wet back. He made him run home in front of the bicycle, as if he were the rancher and his son the naughty bull out of the pen.

The rare days when he caught him, Tamai relished every second. Of course, at home he could flog Pajarito to his heart's content; but making him trot along like that, bringing the whip whistling down on his head, in full view of everyone, the kid publicly humiliated and him firmly reinstated as the head of the family in the neighbors' eyes, delighted one and mortified the other in equal measure.

That's how it had been between them since Pajarito first learned to stand. Maybe they were too alike and the house didn't have space for the pair of them. Instead of being proud of his strapping young son, Tamai was consumed by jealousy and rage. The boy never did as he was told, and worse, his mother always took his side.

As the son grew older, the distance between them widened.

One summer evening, when Pajarito was about twelve, his father was drinking wine on the patio and finished the demijohn. He yelled for his son to get another in town. The kid, just out of the shower, had been about to head into the center to play arcade games with his friends. "Go yourself if you want to keep drinking," he said. Tamai, who'd already had a few too many, seized the rebenque he always kept nearby and went at him. His son raised one arm and the whip encircled him like a wiry snake, he tugged and the braided leather handle burned Tamai's palm. In the minute it took his father to react and get to his feet, Pajarito calmly unwound the whip and got ahold of the handle.

"I'm not your goddamn mencho," he said, and threw it at his feet. Then he turned, got on his bike, and rode away, standing on the pedals.

Marciano had forced himself not to cry when he stood facing his father's coffin.

He would turn twelve the next month, but already he'd smoked his first cigarettes and sucked on the tits of a friend's sister, a sparky fourteen-year-old with chubby cheeks. She didn't let him go any further, though he managed to slip a hand down her panties and stroke her furry pubis, which was warm and soft as a nest.

"Come back for the rest when you're twelve," she said, tucking her tits into her blouse and gently pushing him away.

Marciano had been crossing off the days on the calendar ever since, and as soon as his birthday came, he was going straight back to claim his due. Twelve years exactly from the day he was born, he would become a man.

But he couldn't let himself cry for his father. His father had been killed and he, the eldest of the children, would have to avenge him.

That night, he'd been woken in the early hours by a vehicle parking outside. He got out of bed, peered through the window, and saw the police car. It wasn't unusual for the police to come by at that hour. Miranda was always getting drunk and disorderly in the bars and then being picked up by the cops. Sometimes they left him passed out at the station and sometimes they took him home to his family.

Only the two officers got out. One, who was smoking, leaned against the car door and slowly finished his cigarette. Marciano watched the red embers sharpen and fade with each puff.

Finally they got moving, and after a minute that seemed to go on forever, there came the knocks at the door. Soft knocks, as if they didn't want to be heard. His heart was beating like a snare drum. He stepped into the hallway just as his mother was emerging from her bedroom, in her flip-flops and the faded nightgown she'd bought the last time she gave birth.

"Did you hear knocking?" she asked, her voice thick with sleep.

He said nothing and followed her into the dining room. She switched the light on and Marciano's pupils contracted like a cat's. Estela Miranda opened the front door and saw the policemen. Rebolledo, the one who'd just stubbed out his cigarette, had lit another. Mamani, his colleague, was staring at the ground and didn't even acknowledge the woman's greeting.

"Estela, your husband—" the smoker stammered.

"What's he done now?"

"It's more what he's had done to him."

Rolling over will be a mammoth task. Marciano wants to get his face out of the mud and closer to the cool dawn air, see if he can't suck some of that fresh, newborn air inside himself. Time is precious, they say, but not the paltry sum he has left; loose change at the bottom of a pocket.

Come on, buddy, come on, he thinks.

He remembers his father as if he's right there, cheering for Dago the champion greyhound at the races. Marciano wasn't more than four and Miranda took him everywhere he went: bars, card tables, and the dog track, despite his mother's protests.

"Let him stay here with me, Miranda, go by yourself. Leave the kid alone."

But Miranda lifted him up and put him on the crossbar of his bicycle and took him anyway. Marciano loved being with his father. He gripped the handlebars in his two little hands and felt the hot night air on his face, smelled the Jockeys his old man smoked as they went, which dangled from the corner of his mouth; when they picked up speed, he was like a steam engine. And the smell of aftershave. That was the smell of men.

"Come on, come on, Daguito, you hairy old bastard!" And Miranda would lean right down over the track, shouting at the tiger-striped dog vanishing in the dust behind the mechanical hare.

Come on, kid, you can do it, Marciano tells himself, before slumping spread-eagled back into the mud.

Dago got hit by a car. He'd been roaming around in the street after some bitch. Miranda was lax like that with everything, even things that brought in cash, like the greyhounds. The tendons tore in his right foreleg. Miranda treated it, but to no avail: the animal dragged the injured paw and soon it was infested with maggots. Someone suggested amputating, but Miranda said being crippled was no fit end for a champion. So he decided to put him out of his misery.

One afternoon he took Marciano into the yard, where there was a gnarled old carob tree. He tested one branch with his own weight and tied on a rope. He called the dog over, coaxing, cajoling. Patted his haunches, stroked his head. Then, slowly, he ran the noose around the animal's neck, tightened it, and yanked the other end as hard as he could. The dog whimpered and his three good paws paddled the air, the useless paw fluttering like a rag. And there he stayed, yellow eyes staring up at the leaves.

Marciano felt his eyes stinging and clasped the end of his dick so he wouldn't wet himself. His father carefully lowered Dago to the ground, then crouched and began running his hand down the length of the dog's body.

A neighbor who'd seen what happened from his yard came over to the wire fence.

"You tough bastard, Miranda. Why not just shoot him?"

His father looked up, still stroking the dog. Marciano thought he saw his eyes glisten.

"Stay out of it, okay, or it's you who'll get shot," he said, and bent back down over the animal.

"Come on, come on, you hairy old guy, come on, you can do it! Come on, son!"

Marciano strains to lift his head. He sees his father just a couple of feet away, squatting, a Jockey burning between his lips. The masculine smell fills the morning that's just broken.

"Dad, it's you," he says, though he can't get a word out; he says what he's saying inside his head.

"Dad, it's you. You came to find me," he says, in the same silent speech.

"My son's a champ," he hears his father say, and sees him waving his fists like they're full of betting slips.

"I can't do it, Dad. I can't."

Pajarito feels something warm in his mouth. Warm and soft like the flesh of a ripe papaya plucked off a neighbor's tree. Even if the trees outside his house were heavy with fruit, stolen fruit always tastes sweeter. Sneaking onto patios to pinch papayas. Keeping the scrappy little dogs at bay and hanging from the tree and chucking the spoils to his pal on the other side of the fence.

"Think fast, cocksucker."

Laughing, mouth full, strong and tall until the neighbor looks out, disheveled, blinking away the dregs of siesta.

"Sonofabitch, I'm gonna pump you full of holes!"

Laughing some more and dropping to the ground with a little hop.

"Come on, then, come on, then, you old bastard. Kiss my ass, come on."

And strolling away like he owns the place, while the guy tries to run and do up his trousers and shake his fist all at the same time.

Still laughing with his friend in the middle of the street. And if the owner of the papayas is looking for a fight and follows them onto the sidewalk, lobbing the fruit in his face.

"Eat this, you cheap motherfucker! Want your papayas? Here you go, and here."

How do heads even work. The stuff you end up thinking, the stuff that comes back. He smiles.

He touches his parched lip with the tip of his tongue.

Warm and soft and sweet like . . .

If anyone had told him, hinted, even, he'd have spat on them first and then beaten them to a pulp. And yet. It was like having a live baby animal in his mouth.

"Slowly now, Pájaro. Get it all in. That's it, nice and slow, watch those teeth. That's it, baby, that's it."

The Tamais had married young and with family on the way. Before saying yes to the priest, Celina had said yes to her boyfriend, to the urgency of his kisses that left her neck and shoulders covered in tiny bruises. Which was also like saying no to her father, who disapproved of the relationship.

The first time was uncomfortable and painful, a far cry from the Corín Tellado stories that fueled her teenage fantasies. They'd done it in the middle of a dance, at the Húngaro. After the DJ stopped playing the latest hits and put on some milongas and chamamés for the older couples and the mothers and aunts who were there as chaperones, and before the live band showed up.

Tamai took Celina by the arm and led her from the dance. They emerged into the warm night and made their way through the parked cars. Celina glimpsed arms and legs moving inside some of the vehicles, blurry behind the steamed-up glass: privileged girls who at least had a private cubicle in which to give themselves away.

They reached a cluster of trees and Tamai leaned her against a trunk. She felt the rough bark scratching her back, which her summer dress left bare. She clutched her panties in one fist, and the other she bit so as not to cry out when her boyfriend pushed all the way inside her.

When it was over, she rearranged her clothes in a daze. Tamai, panting, fell back against the tree and lit a cigarette, then pulled her in with one arm and kissed her on the forehead.

"Can't get pregnant standing up," he murmured.

Estela Miranda woke before dawn. She'd been dreaming about carnival. It was the end of December, and the night before, she'd been up late embroidering costumes for the Ara Sunú dance troupe. In her dream, despite being pregnant, she was the queen again. Dancing on the float in very high heels, a bra and miniskirt, the gold lamé cloak, and the crown perched on her short hair. Her whole body, including her belly, was covered in glitter. From her position on the trailer–turned–royal carriage, she saw some kids approaching with water balloons in their hands. Against carnival rules—don't get the queen wet—the boys took aim with their liquid grenades, and the multicolored balloons hit their target, soaking her from head to toe.

Far from annoyed, Estela, who'd been the Ara Sunú queen at several carnivals running and knew her way around the royal airs and graces, smiled and silently threatened them with her scepter, shaking her hips all the while to the rhythm of the drums.

When she woke and sat up in bed, there was still a smile on her lips, the smile that had been photographed by every newspaper in the region. She switched on the lamp and when she pulled back the sheets, a few sequins went flying; she must have carried them into bed with her after all the hours of embroidery. Her water had broken, and the mattress underneath her was sopping wet. The other side was dry and empty. Miranda was off playing Mus, which he did every night, at the Imperio bar.

She felt her heart beating harder. But from joy, not fear. She knew exactly what she had to do: get dressed, grab the little bag she'd packed weeks ago, leave a note for her husband, walk the two blocks to the neighbor who had a phone—she was expecting her, and knew Estela might come knocking at any time of the day or night and ask her to call a taxi—and take a towel, too, to put on the car seat so she didn't dirty the upholstery. She'd been keeping the money for the journey separate in her purse.

Everything happened just the way she'd planned. Never letting her carnival-queen smile falter, she bore the first pains, which came as she was at her neighbor's, waiting for the car. The woman offered to go with her to the hospital, but Estela said no, she should go back to bed, she'd already done enough.

Estela Miranda knew full well: although you make children with somebody else, you bring them into the world alone.

Oscar Tamai came to the town to work the cotton harvest. If anyone had seen him getting off the train with the hundreds of other pickers who showed up every day, he'd have struck them as different from the rest. Oscar Tamai turned heads. Back then he was a handsome young man, of average height, with indio eyes and a black mustache that curled down at the corners of his mouth. He wore a sombrero and cowboy boots and looked like a gunslinger straight out of the *D'Artagnan* comic books. But it wasn't his good looks that marked him out so much as his insolence. His way of standing, of moving, of looking around with a slight jerk of the head, narrowing his eyes until they were just two cracks, two holes stabbed in a can—these things all set him apart from the other migrant workers, men worn down by poverty and hard manual labor, mostly indigenous, silent, and ashamed.

In his free time he stopped by the bar across from the train station, like all the other pickers. It was where the cotton farmers went to round up laborers to work in their fields.

The bar was a family business, run by a Catalan widower and his three daughters. Two pushing thirty and the youngest, Celina, just sixteen. The older girls mostly handled the cooking, while the father and Celina served customers and worked the cash register.

The first time Oscar Tamai set foot in the bar, Celina was drying some glasses behind the counter. As soon as he entered the gloomy space, the blades of the ceiling fan circling lazily, the evening sun filtering through the door and lighting him from behind, picking out the shape of his sombrero, his yellow eyes adjusting to the dim interior, she felt her heart stop in her chest.

But only for a moment, because when the man came walking toward her, his boot steps echoing on the floor tiles, it started beating wildly. Tamtam, went the boots; tamtamtam, went her heart.

Celina was beginning to think her sisters' fate would be hers, too, could see herself yellowing in the bar's stale air, stooping in the mighty shadow of her father, who thought the only man worthy of his daughters was himself. With the other two, he'd scared away the suitors until the girls gave up and stopped looking. Convinced as well, in the end, that no man could ever be good enough.

Although she'd sworn not to end up like the elder pair, at times she felt hopeless. How could she ever get a man if she spent all her waking hours surrounded by drunken indios?

Tamai greeted her, touching the brim of his hat, and asked for a beer. Instead of going to sit down, he stayed leaning on the counter as he waited for the drink. Her hands shook when she passed him the bottle and glass. He paid, said thanks, and went to sit at a table by the window.

At that time the bar was almost empty. Oscar Tamai turned his chair toward the counter and stretched out his legs, one foot on top of the other, one thumb hooked in his belt loop and that hand resting on his crotch, his other hand moving between cigarette and glass, his hat tilted slightly over his forehead. Celina couldn't see his eyes, but she felt the man's gaze, how it sought her like a knife thrower's blades.

She knew instantly that this newcomer was the man she'd been waiting for. She also knew her father would throw a fit.

That day, he finished his beer and left. He came back again the following days, though he stopped coming up to the counter, instead sitting at his usual table and waiting for her to bring his order. He began by brushing her fingers when he passed her the cash, and her hand or arm when she set the bottle on the table. Eventually she leaned so close he could brush against her breast, the nipple bare under her dress.

Pajarito coughs and that soft warm sweet whatever leaves his mouth. He wipes his chin with his hand, then holds his palm above his face, moving it closer, farther away, trying to focus. The sky white and his palm so red.

His eyes fill with tears that trickle from the corners, seeping all the way behind his ears. He lets his arm drop, rests his palm in the mud. His other hand, ever since he fell, has been under the waistband of his jeans. He doesn't need to look to know blood's coming out there too. His fingers are sticky.

When Marciano pulled out the knife from inside him, even with the shouting, the frantic running around, and the shots fired by their friends on both sides, even with all that commotion and the music still going, Pajarito heard clear as day the fffshshshhhh that came from the hole, as if his belly were a deflating balloon.

The other guy couldn't be much better off. He'd managed to stab him a couple of times. If he were doing any better, he'd have come back to finish the job. Either he was dead already or he was getting there, like him.

And the guys? Cardozo, Nango, and Josecito? Where've they all gone? Why didn't the police come, or the ambulance?

He squints and a tune starts to play. A sexy cumbia track that spreads through the club. Everyone's gone off to dance, to pick someone up they can screw later on. Not him. He's not feeling it.

He sits alone on a tabletop nursing his beer, watching the dancing from the sidelines. The chicks still put on a show for him. He sees Rosana, Vero, and Vero's cousin dancing together and all three girls are giving him the eye. Soon the other girl joins them, the blonde the guys call Vieja de Agua, after the fish that's so gross you can eat only the tail. She's as ugly as sin, the gringa, but she has a big round ass like the full moon. And, as if in honor of her nickname, she's the only one of the four who lets you do her up the butt.

As if she knows her ass is the only thing going for her, the gringa dances with her back to him the whole time. The white miniskirt squeezes her curves and where her crack ends you can see the little triangle of her thong. Pájaro chuckles. Who knows, maybe he'll work up an appetite after all.

He takes a swig. The beer's warm, so he spits it out and chucks the bottle and goes to the bar for another. He weaves through the crowd, shouldering wet bodies aside.

"Hey, man, how 'bout a cold one this time . . . That last bottle was more like piss water."

"What d'you expect, man, it's fucking baking. They're cold when I get them out."

"Oh, sure, sure. Do I look like a sucker to you?"

He takes the bottle, pays, and leaves. At least there's a warmish breeze outside.

The music is fading gradually, drifting away like it's all happening someplace else. The lukewarm air turns cold and he's back sprawled on the grass, empty-handed and alone, feeling himself sliding into a bottomless pit.

"Are you still there, Dad?" Marciano says the words inside his head.

Where's his dad gone, why's he left him alone again. He needs to sit up somehow, needs to get to his feet and look for his dad now that he's back. Knowing Miranda, he'll be getting his fix at the shooting gallery or that game where you throw the hoops. With the fair to himself, he won't rest till he's won the grand prize, the giant teddy bear, lumpy and discolored from waiting so long for someone to score a bull's-eye and carry it off. Not that it's about the prize; it's the buzz from playing that counts.

He tries to move and can't do it, and as he's about to give up, he feels himself being lifted gently by the shoulders, turned over, and laid on his back on the ground. He blinks several times. First he sees the sky, completely white, and then his father's smiling face.

"Dad, you came back."

Miranda is sitting on the ground, supporting his son in his lap, Marciano's head resting on one of his father's legs. He shifts so they can see each other.

Around his neck, his father has the same silk scarf he was buried in. He unties it and uses it to wipe the mud from his son's face. Marciano's cheeks feel cool now, his eyes clear. For the first time, he can see the wound at his father's throat. It's just like he imagined: a wide gash the whole way across, clumsily sewn up by the funeral home staff. Like a second mouth, bigger than the first and grinning.

Estela put the scarf around his neck to stop nosy onlookers from gawking at the wound. She knew that once word got out about how Miranda died, people would flock to the vigil just to see it. And spiteful as people are, they made stuff up even so: that at one point the scarf had slipped and they'd caught a glimpse of the gash; that it wasn't just a cut but a clean slice separating the head from the body, and to hide it and keep the head from bouncing around in the coffin they'd used long pins to attach it to the shroud. Marciano had to listen to crap like this the whole year after his father's murder, and because of crap like this he'd wound up in fistfights almost every day with almost every other kid at school.

"Does it hurt, Dad?"

Miranda roars with laughter, throwing his head back. In the white light Marciano sees, clearly, the dry scab covering the wound.

"Nothing can hurt me. You're the one who's falling to pieces, son."

Marciano smiles.

"You got a cigarette?"

Miranda glances at him, surprised. Then he smiles and winks. His eyes are dancing.

"If your mom finds out, there'll be hell to pay. You know how she is."

He thinks for a second, shrugs, gets out a cigarette, and lights it.

"You're old enough to smoke now. But best not to mention it, 'cause she won't be happy with me."

He takes a drag first, a deep lungful before blowing out

the thick smoke, then puts the cigarette between his son's lips. Marciano breathes in and feels the slight dizziness of the morning's first cigarette.

He's smoking with his dad. It's not too late for some things after all.

"And what are you going to call him?" the nurse asked, helping her latch the baby onto her breast.

"Marciano," Estela said, looking at her son's round face under the shock of jet-black hair.

The nurse laughed.

"That's no name for a Christian, dear. Call him Ángel, like the guy in the telenovela. Lots of people are choosing it these days, and it's so pretty."

Estela smiled. He was going to be called Marciano.

"Do you have a husband?"

She nodded.

"Well," said the nurse, checking her watch, "I'm off to drink some maté before Rosita gets here. I'll leave the cleaning to her. I don't get a wink of sleep these days, the rate folks are popping them out."

The nurse shuffled out in her white clogs, leaving Estela alone at last with her baby boy.

The dawn light came in through the windows of the maternity ward. Almost all the beds, perhaps twenty or so, were full. The new mothers' bodies formed white mounds under the sheets. Next to each bed stood a little iron crib with peeling paintwork, just like hers. No, not next to each bed: there were two beds with nothing, and Estela, who couldn't see the women, imagined them awake, their eyes fixed on the ceiling. Their babies had died. Estela hugged hers closer to her chest and then lifted the blanket to see the whole of him, counting his tiny fingers and toes.

Miranda showed up at the hospital at two in the afternoon, visiting hours. He'd showered, shaved, and changed into clean clothes. He gave his wife a kiss and then stood by her bed, uncertain.

The ward was beginning to fill up. One group looked like they'd come for a picnic, spreading maté gourds and biscuits over the new mother's bed.

Estela pointed to the crib.

"It's your son, Miranda. Pick him up."

Miranda peered down. He was nervous. He turned away, wiped his hands on his trousers, then pulled back the sheet and lifted the boy up.

"Support his head with your arm."

The man laughed.

"He's like a little howler monkey, look at all that hair."

Estela smiled, too, and patted the side of the bed, motioning for the new father to sit.

Her husband could be a bit of a mess, but when it came down to it, Estela thought, he'd be a good dad.

The nurse was right: the registry's office wouldn't let them call him Marciano. Miranda put him down with his grandpa's name instead, but only for the paperwork, because everyone was going to call him Marciano, just like his mother wanted.

Estela and Celina just missed each other in the maternity ward. When Estela was taking her newborn son home, Celina was on her way in with the early pains. This was her second child. Her first had been born a little over a year ago. Even then she was a pro at giving birth: a few contractions not much worse than a bellyache and then the baby slid right out. According to the midwife, the mother's wide hips had made the job easier. It was the same this time. The nurse had barely gotten her shaved before the kid was out and bawling.

"Is it a boy?" she asked, and when the midwife said yes and showed her, Celina fell back into the delivery chair, relieved and happy.

She'd been disappointed when her first was a girl. She was scared of being like her mother and having only daughters. Her whole life she'd longed for a brother, and when she was ready to have children, all she wanted was to give birth to a son.

The baby was a bundle of energy. He never stopped waving his tiny arms, as if flapping a pair of wings.

"He's like a little bird," Celina said with a smile. And although she'd had a name in mind since her first pregnancy, she began to call him just that: Pajarito.

Tamai was also pleased it was a boy. He adored his daughter, Sonia, but he wanted a man, a continuation of himself, his surname and his ways. That day, when he went to see his son and held him in his arms, a scrap of fidgety brown flesh, he never dreamed he'd grow to be so like himself that they'd end up hating each other. Or that the kid would replace him so completely in his wife's heart.

Taking up with Tamai had earned Celina the scorn of her father and sisters. The old man would never forgive her for surrendering her virtue to some lousy, dirt-poor cotton-picker, a half indio with no family to speak of, and who was cocky as hell to top it off.

Her sisters would never forgive her for the thrill of having a man inside her, on top of her, filling all her holes. "Why her and not us?" they seemed to say, eyes clouded with envy, lips shut tight, and legs, too, for good measure, so that Yasi Yateré satyr didn't knock them up as well just by looking at them.

Since Celina was a minor, they couldn't get married by law, but they called in at the chapel of a priest, who agreed to bless their union because a baby was on the way. Tamai was no believer, but he went along with the charade to put her mind at ease.

She left her house with what she had on: her old man hadn't even let her pack her clothes.

Celina had no idea what Tamai's plans were for after the harvest. She didn't know where her man had come from or where he was headed. They'd never exactly talked much, aside from lovers' chitchat. But she didn't care.

After that first time at the Húngaro, muddled and quick, they'd carried on practicing and Celina soon got a taste for that violent, unfettered kind of loving, of fucking nonstop, of straddling Tamai's hips and crying out for him to fill her again and again.

Celina married for love and the love lasted until her little boy was born. And she realized this that same afternoon, during visiting hours, when she saw the kid in her husband's arms. Right away, her eyes welled up and she looked at Tamai like they were saying goodbye, the two of them on the platform and him about to board the train he'd ridden in on, about to disappear forever.

If before there was room in her heart for a man of five feet six and a hundred and eighty pounds, now, in the same space, all she could fit was that handful of flesh that waved its arms and legs as if flapping its wings, just like a little bird.

He can't bring himself to ask his dad how it happened. There's no one better to explain the whole thing from start to finish, but he just can't. His dad looks so carefree with his son's head in his lap, stroking his muddy hair, smiling down at him as he pulls on the cigarette and blows out the white smoke, which rises and fades in the white sky.

He reconstructs the scene for the millionth time.

The two policemen at the door in the middle of the night, his mother in a nightgown, one hand gripping the doorframe, the other stroking her hair flirtatiously. Him behind her, in his underwear, barefoot and ribs sticking out, a kid in a growth spurt who hasn't yet learned to manage his gangly frame.

His mother asking what her husband's done now to make them come knocking, sounding more reproachful of the cops than of her husband. Did they really need to drive all the way here at this hour? Why not let him sleep it off in a cell like the other times?

Then one of the pigs saying Miranda hasn't done anything, that what's been done was done to him and there's no changing it now. That Elvio Miranda is dead, he's been killed. Did they say like a dog or did he hear that later, from everyone else?

He can't see his mother's face, because she has her back to him, but he sees her bow her head and wrap her arms around her body; he doesn't hear her cry, but he sees her faded nightgown begin to tremble, convulsing with her flesh. The policeman who'd spoken takes a step into the house, leans forward, and gives his mother a hug. Then he sees Marciano and shakes his head. "What are you doing there, buddy?" he says, and, still patting his mother on the shoulder, glances behind him and tells the other cop, who's waiting on the porch: "One of the kids is here."

But when he looks again, there's no one. Marciano has gone back to bed, pulled the sheets right up, and buried his face in the pillow because he's asleep, yes, that's it, he's asleep and having a horrible nightmare: the police have come to say his dad's been killed. His dad'll find it hilarious tomorrow when he tells him, when the sun's high in the sky and the two of them are sitting in the yard under the awning, Marciano drinking his glass of milk and Miranda his Gancia with ice. They'll both find it hilarious.

"Thanks, son," his father will say. "Always looking out for me."

Not long after Pajarito was born, Tamai was offered some work. At the time they were living in a tiny rented room with a shared bathroom, which they could only just afford.

Tamai did odd jobs. In the cotton fields during the harvest, and the rest of the year, whatever came up: loading and unloading building materials, installing wire fences in the fields, cutting back trees in the town, laboring on construction sites. He went from one job to another, with no interest in finding something steady. Whenever Celina told him to put his name down with the council—they always needed people and that was a secure job, a job for life—he'd make excuses, and if she pushed him, they'd end up fighting, with Tamai saying he'd never be a government mencho, he was meant for other things, meant to be free as a bird, and then storming out, slamming the door, to vent his frustration at some bar.

There, his buddies rallied around him. While buying one another drinks, they exchanged tips on how to treat women so they'd stay in line and know their place.

Celina had gone out to work as soon as she shacked up with Tamai. She cleaned houses and did people's laundry. Food and bills were paid mostly with what she earned, since nearly all his wages went to his benders.

The offer of work that came, the only proper work Tamai would have for as long as the marriage lasted, came thanks to her.

A friend's relative, a brickmaker, was moving south, where apparently good jobs were to be had with the oil companies. He was leaving a functioning brick kiln and a basic house on the same land: two bedrooms, a kitchen, and a bathroom. All he wanted in return was a bit of rent to send to his elderly mother. The girl told Celina the brickworks were doing well, that her relative worked there alone and got by fine, that this was a good opportunity. Plenty of buildings were going up in the area and everyone was buying bricks. The kiln could make you enough to pay the rent and have something left over to live on.

Celina was eager from the get-go. Maybe this was what her husband needed: a job where he could be his own boss.

Tamai knew nothing about making bricks, but he could learn: he was a smart guy, and from what her friend had said, making bricks wasn't exactly a science. She could even lend a hand and stop scrubbing other people's filth once and for all.

Before speaking to him—she knew what he was like and knew it was better to wait till everything was sorted out—Celina asked her friend to take her to see the brickmaker.

The kiln was in La Cruceña, the oldest neighborhood in town, built around the old tannin extraction plant. The houses, dating back to 1900, were falling apart, but there were still people living in all of them. The two women walked down the dirt roads, where dogs and barefoot children played; there were horses loose in the empty lots, and goats in pens. It wasn't the best neighborhood in town, but it wasn't the worst, either.

The brickmaker came out to greet them when he heard the dogs barking. He wore shorts and nothing else, but upon seeing his cousin arriving with another woman, he ducked back inside and reappeared in a half-buttoned shirt.

The man lived alone. He offered his hand to Celina, a rough hand, ravaged by work. They sat under the awning, a roof of twisted gray stems with a few green leaves, which Celina recognized as a trumpet vine in need of water and attention.

While her friend caught him up on some family business, Celina looked around. It all seemed pretty grim: the ground dotted with huge craters where the raw materials for making bricks had been dug out, the house a lot more basic than she'd imagined. Still, she held fast to her optimism and told herself it just needed a woman's touch: curtains in the windows, a good cleaning, and plants, lots of plants to keep it from looking as bare as the surface of the moon.

Eventually her friend explained why she and Celina were there. The relative, a man of few words, nodded and said he wasn't looking to sell for the time being, at least not till he was sure of his job down south, but he didn't want to leave the place empty, either, in case people broke in. They discussed the rent, and Celina, a salesman's daughter, haggled until the man agreed to lower it to what she had in mind.

They said goodbye, shaking hands again, and she promised to return with Tamai so the man could teach him the trade.

She felt happy. Not only was Pajarito the light of her life, but he'd come into the world with some bread tucked under his arm.

Elvio Miranda came from a brickmaking family. His grandfather was one of the first in the trade and used to brag that much of the town had been built with his bricks. He said that even the factory chimney in La Cruceña, which was more than 130 feet tall, had been made using bricks from his kiln. This older Miranda had amassed a small fortune, which Elvio's father then set about squandering. Elvio had inherited the remains of one of the five brickworks the family used to own, and the addictions of his father.

Elvio Miranda liked his trade, but more than anything else he liked betting.

That was the man Estela met: a gambler, a charmer, and a slacker. And she, the carnival queen, the girl who could have had her pick of guys, chose him. Her godmother, Señora Nena, the woman who raised her, shook her head when Estela told her who she'd fallen in love with. But Señora Nena, who'd come down from Brazil two decades before to settle there on that northern plain, and who, malicious rumor had it, was a woman with a salacious past ("Past! Present more like, my darling," she'd say with a cackle if anyone brought up the gossip), encouraged her in the romance. Estela wouldn't have a secure economic future with Miranda, but she'd have a hell of a lot of fun, thought Señora Nena, who had a soft spot for feckless types like Elvio Miranda.

And so they were married after a brief engagement, and

Señora Nena gifted them a trip to Los Cocos, in Córdoba province. Before the wedding, Miranda persuaded her to leave her job as an accountant's secretary. When they were back from their honeymoon, they settled in the brickworks on the outskirts of La Cruceña, a hundred yards from the other brickworks, where, not long after, the Tamais would move in.

There being no witnesses, the police had to reconstruct the scene of the crime. Elvio Miranda left the Imperio at three in the morning after a bad run of cards (another five minutes and he'd have bet his own wife, his gambling buddies said).

The murderers—and the police assumed it was murderers plural—waited across the road from the bar, hiding in a half-built house (the proof being the large pile of cigarette butts later found there), and followed him at a distance. When Miranda left the well-lit area around the Imperio and turned down the straight road that would take him home, they shot him in the back.

Miranda fell facedown on the sidewalk, wounded but not dead. One of the guys walked over and stamped on him, hard, with one foot, to hold him still (hence the bruising around the kidneys), yanked back his hair with one hand, and used the knife in the other to slit his throat.

Then they were gone.

Night's closing in, Pájaro, he thinks, and half smiles, because what kind of night would show its face with a sky as white as this one? But obviously it means something else. He has to keep his mind going till help arrives. He can't think of a way out of this. He has to project memories onto that white sky that looks so much like the screen at the Cervantes and hold on to them tight.

Come on, Pájaro, come on, remember something.

His father's not what he'd have picked, but the fucker's here anyway. Never mind, kid, never mind, go with it. Besides, it's good to remember his dad now, because the memory lights a fire in his gut, a burning rage, an urge to track him down and smash his face in now that he could, now that he's grown up and could beat him senseless without breaking a sweat. Good thing his dad's here: hating him is fuel. Think of him and throw more wood on the fire, don't let it go out, keep it nice and warm, because now and then he gets this cold feeling inside.

How's the old man doing? Where is he these days?

Not a single worthwhile memory. He was scared of him, though he never showed it. His father thought he defied him, but no: it was pure fear, fear that came out that way, like when a cornered animal attacks. Deep down, he was scared shitless. And when he stopped being scared, when he found the courage to take him on, the low-rent bum walks out and leaves him hanging. He disappears and Pájaro is stuck with all that rage hammering inside his head, loud and pointless as an empty shotgun.

When he was finally ready to rip him a new one, the mother-fucker ups and leaves. He couldn't let him have even that satisfaction.

At first he was over the moon, why deny it? His mom taking him aside, telling him Tamai had gone. Him not believing his luck, asking where to, how long for. Her shaking her head, lowering her gaze, eyeing her ringless hands. She'd had a ring once, a gold band that glinted in the sun and that she took off only when she used it to treat their sties. Her husband bought it for her one time after a big win. He'd shown up at around ten that morning, blind drunk. Celina was waiting in the doorway with a litany of complaints, but before she could open her mouth, Tamai produced the little box lined with red fabric and gave her the ring.

She'd always wanted a ring that would show the world she was married, so her excitement overcame her irritation and she even followed him inside and helped him lie down and tucked him in like a child and sat on the edge of the bed, sliding the ring onto each finger in turn till he started to snore. She had it a few years. When she was anxious or worried or deep in thought, she twisted it on her middle finger with her thumb. One morning she woke up and didn't need to look to know that something was missing. Her husband had taken her ring as she slept, to pawn or send spinning over the card table's green cloth.

Still, she kept the habit of rubbing her thumb and middle finger when she was worried. That day, Pajarito clearly remembers, when he asked how long for, she made that same movement and said: "Forever." She didn't look sad. Thoughtful, maybe.

"You're the man of the house now," she told him, ruffling his hair. "We'll make it work together, you and me."

Pajarito, who was maybe thirteen, nodded yes, but didn't let on how happy he was. He adored his mother, and, after all, she'd just lost her husband.

It wasn't till a few days later that he realized his father had stuck it to him again. Now that he was finally ready to smash his face in, the goddamn sonofabitch was gone.

Oscar Tamai began making bricks a month after Celina came to terms with the owner of the kiln. He was a smart guy and soon got the hang of the work, though he wasn't happy about it.

At first, and given how Celina sold him on the idea, he'd jumped at the chance: being his own boss and working the hours he chose were things he'd always wanted. No one ordering him around or walking all over him: he, Oscar Tamai, master of his destiny again—it was going to be beautiful.

But once they moved to the brickworks, he realized he'd have his wife around morning, noon, and night, Celina and the kids under his feet from the moment he got up till he went to bed, and all the domestic problems. All the stuff he used to escape, with the excuse of doing odd jobs or going out to look for them; a married man's routine, which he'd always steered clear of before.

He'd be his own boss, but Celina, he could tell, would be worse than any of the slave drivers he'd come across in his time.

If a boss got his back up, Oscar Tamai used to quit on the spot and get the hell out. He felt on top of the world when he did it, when someone pushed him too far, biting the hand that fed him like the wily cur he was. Shouting louder than the boss, telling him to go fuck himself, and then taking his time walking out, boots coming down hard, owning every step, the other workers following the scene with their heads bowed, but, Tamai knew, congratulating him inside, saying from inside their gritted teeth: "That Tamai has some fucking balls."

Then straight to the bar to tell the tale, to spread his free spirit around the others, the others who'd never have had the nerve. And from the bar, emboldened by drink, going home to empty that massive pair of balls into his wife.

Now none of that would be possible. Celina, the old trout, had sold him up the river. Every day now a copy of the last: back broken by wheelbarrows full of wood, bent double in the muddy pisadero, sweating like a pig over piles of burning bricks.

Although it would be a few years before he finally made up his mind, even then, a month after laying the first brick of the stable life Celina wanted for herself and her children, Oscar Tamai was thinking about ditching it all.

If she began her goodbyes when Pajarito was born, he began his in the remorseless midday sun, leaning on his shovel, feet buried in the mud, back muscles on fire, eyes two hate-filled slits.

Some months after they became neighbors, Elvio Miranda showed up at Tamai's brickworks—which everyone still thought of as Leyes's brickworks, after the last owner, who was still the owner, bah, to the tenant's profound irritation: "It's Tamai's brickworks now," he'd snap testily whenever someone came by asking for Leyes.

Miranda clapped to make himself known, though he was already through the little wire gate that separated the property from the street.

It was getting dark, but the heat hadn't let up a whisker. Under the awning, with no lights on so as not to attract the nighttime bugs, Tamai was sitting in a beach chair.

"Come in," he yelled, without getting up.

Miranda made his way over the uneven patio. Although everything was switched off, the evening glow of the sky made it easy enough to see.

"'Scuse me," said the visitor.

"Bit late for that," Tamai answered, leaning slightly forward.

Miranda thought he was getting up to greet him, but no. Instead he stretched out an arm for a tin cup that was on the table. He took a swig and set it on the ground, closer to himself, and wiped his mouth with his hand. The same hand then moved to stroke the head of the puppy in his lap.

He didn't ask the visitor to sit down, or offer any pleasantries. Miranda stayed on his feet and lit a cigarette, for something to do.

"Listen, Tamai, that dog's mine."

Tamai smiled and turned his full attention back to the little animal. A long-nosed greyhound, with dark stripes and ears still too big for its skull, the tail a thin snake slapping against the man's thigh. He put a finger in its mouth, the needlelike teeth clamped down on his calloused skin, and it swung its head from side to side, not letting go. Tamai smiled again and held the dog up to his face and it licked his nose. He liked that milky smell puppies have.

"I think you're mistaken," he said.

"It's my dog. A neighbor saw you take it."

"You're telling me I'm a thief."

"I'm telling you to give it back. It's a racing dog. From Daisy's litter. The sire and dam are champions, you hear?"

"This is my dog," he said, and leaned forward to take another swig.

"Cut the bullshit, Tamai. Give it back."

Tamai chuckled.

"I don't want any trouble, Tamai."

"You don't want any trouble, but you show up at my house saying I stole one of your dogs. That's funny. If I don't want any trouble, I stay at home."

"This isn't just any dog, okay? It's a future champion. The best of the litter. If you want a puppy, I'll give you another one. But not this one."

"I don't want a dog. I've got one already."

"These aren't ordinary dogs. They need special care. Training. Understand?"

Tamai lifted the puppy with one hand and moved it this way and that in the air. It whimpered.

43

"Doesn't look so special to me. It's a dog. Bit skinny, sure. You can tell the last owner was stingy with the food. It's not nice to mistreat animals, don't you agree?"

Miranda's laugh couldn't hide his powerlessness.

"Fine. If the dog's yours, I'll buy it off you. How much d'you want?"

"No, Miranda. This dog's not for sale. It belongs to Sonia, my little girl. Imagine how upset she'd be if I let it go. She's fond of it."

Miranda lit another cigarette. His mouth was dry. He glanced up, the sky visible through the bare thatch of the awning. It was completely dark now, but there were stars. As he wondered what else he could say to change Tamai's mind, the gate creaked open. He looked over his shoulder and saw Tamai's wife coming in, holding the baby in one arm and the little girl by the hand.

"Evening," the woman said.

"Ma'am . . . ," Miranda greeted her.

The girl, just two years old, waddled toward her dad with the duck-like gait of children new to walking, and hugged the little puppy.

"What'd I tell you," said Tamai, and he lifted the girl onto his lap.

"Fine," said Miranda, stamping out his cigarette. "But look after it. Take it to the vet in town, they'll tell you how to raise it. It's a good dog, Tamai, make the most of it."

He turned and left the way he'd come.

Officially, the two men's feud began with the stolen puppy, but it had been brewing even before they were neighbors. Neither was sure how it started. One of those nights when they were hanging around in some bar till the early hours, they'd had an altercation. About what, neither could remember. The picture they had was hazy: they'd been at one of those big tables with the usual bunch of layabouts, talking about this or that, when one of them made some comment and the other took it wrong, then they were on their feet, chairs skidding back, and their pals all fell silent; they faced each other in the stale air, eyes bloodshot and fists ready to land.

But they were plastered, and a voice of reason on each side told them to cut it out. Their pals had made them sit down and called for more drinks, and calm was restored, a veil drawn over the whole thing, putting out the spark before it became a blaze. And so the two men forgot, yes, why they'd been so angry, but they didn't forget they had unfinished business.

Swiping the puppy was Tamai's way of bringing that old grudge up-to-date. Now, with the two men neighbors, and both brickmakers, too, the gloves would well and truly come off.

When he left his neighbor's place, Miranda was sure Tamai would train the dog and pit it against one of his on the track. He hadn't been lying when he'd said that puppy was the best of the litter. Miranda knew more about greyhounds than about anything else, and while the bitch birthed the litter, he'd been mentally marking the champions from the rest.

He resolved to train the remaining pups triply hard so he wouldn't be shown up the day they went head-to-head.

But Tamai had other plans. He liked betting, but he didn't have the patience to train a dog. He'd taken it to screw with him, that was all, and he wasn't done yet.

So as the months went by, Miranda had to watch as Tamai ruined his dog. Skinny, chained to a post in the yard, tongue hanging out on those days when the heat cracked the earth. Turned vicious by its owner's punishments. Roaming around the neighborhood, stealing food from the trash, fighting other dogs, coat raw with scars and insect bites. Running after the cars: a shadow of the animal's former aerodynamic grace.

His heart broke every time he caught sight of it. Sometimes he wished it were left chained up so he wouldn't have to watch the creature's slow decline.

Estela couldn't bear to see her husband so torn up about the dog.

One night, when everyone was asleep, she snuck through the

yards of the other houses on the block until she reached Tamai's. The greyhound was tied to the usual post. It was easy to keep it quiet with a bit of food. A couple of pieces first, as bait, then a big ball of meat mixed with ground glass. She was shaking all the way home. Horrified at what she'd just done, but comforted to think that now the greyhound would stop suffering, too, the poor thing.

Pajarito remembers. He remembers everything now, the memories come at him like sucker punches, thick and fast, in no particular order.

He's ten years old again. Standing stiffly, furrowing his brow, next to the display table with the big glass fish tank. His mother's dressed him in his best clothes: navy blue pants from his communion that are now too tight, the crotch strangling his balls, not to mention too short, the hem hovering above his ankles even though his mom's let it out all the way; a flannel shirt, red, green, and black check, which he likes, it's new, trendy—there was enough money for a new shirt, but not for pants; his newest sneakers, a pair of canvas Flechas, also blue; and his hair neatly combed to one side.

He sneaks a glance at the fish tank, which is lit by a spotlight from above: the fish with both eyes on one side of its head swims about in the water, between the glass walls, looking for the way back to the canal where Pajarito trapped it the day before. He feels like escaping as well, joining everyone else on the other side of the closed doors, in the hustle and bustle, away from the rancid stillness of the museum.

"All set, kiddo?" the attendant asks, and the attendant's wife smiles at him from a distance.

Pajarito nods and the attendant snaps his fingers, taking his place on the other side of the fish tank just as the double doors swing open and people start pushing their way in. A thick cord keeps the onlookers from getting too close. When the photographers start snapping, the flashes blind him. For a moment, everything looks white.

The attendant calls for quiet and says a few words. Pajarito doesn't listen, he's scanning the crowd for people he knows, he spots some kids from school who make faces at him, and sees his mother and siblings off to one side. He looks for his father, but doesn't see him.

He jumps when the attendant takes him by the shoulders and pulls him nearer, hears him asking for a round of applause, and then the clapping, the murmur that swells, then some bigger kid who yells from the back, "Hey, Pajarito, nice ankles!" and the chorus of laughs, the attendant leading him out of the spotlight, the museum staff lifting the cord and everyone pushing and shoving once more to see the freakish specimen up close.

"Well done, kid, well done," the attendant says, patting his cheek, then he takes his wife by the arm and they disappear into the throng.

Pajarito is left alone and kind of disoriented. With two fingers he tugs at his crotch, trying to stop the seams from pinching his balls. He wants to go home and take those crappy pants off. He makes his way through the crowd and when he finally reaches the sidewalk, the people waiting there recognize him—"It's the kid who caught the fish!"—and then comes a rush of questions: Where did he catch it, does it really have two eyes on the same side, does it have square teeth like a Christian, does it this, that, and the other.

Pajarito doesn't know, doesn't answer, he shrugs and just wants to be out of there. "Cat's got his tongue," someone says, and the others laugh gleefully. "Stand up straight, you rude boy," an old lady adds, "and speak when you're spoken to." Another woman says: "You can tell he's Tamai's son, the stuck-up little brat."

He's mortified and runs away, runs the six or seven blocks between there and his house, then stops at the gate to catch his breath. The sun's going down and the house is in semidarkness, but he sees the glow of his father's cigarette that rises and falls under the awning, like a tiny will-o'-the-wisp.

He goes in. Tamai is drinking wine from his tin cup.

"They done going gaga over that fish yet?" he asks.

Pajarito says nothing. He's not going to answer these questions either.

"Folks have too much time on their hands in this goddamn town."

The kid turns to head into the house, but Tamai's voice stops him.

"Sit down."

"I'm going in to change my pants."

"I said sit down," he repeats, and kicks a chair out from under the table. "What's the problem? Too high and mighty to sit with your old man for a bit?"

Pajarito sits.

"That's more like it."

Tamai sparks another cigarette, and Pajarito sees his face lit up by the darting flame. He feels frightened, contemptuous.

"They give you anything?"

"Huh?"

"Did they give you anything for the fish? Any cash?"

"No."

"Not exactly a genius, are you? They should've given you a few pesos for that fish. Or d'you think the dog shits golden eggs around here? Carrying on like you're a millionaire, giving charity handouts to the council. It's all your mother's fault for spoiling you. I'd been working in the fields for years by the time I was your age, let me tell you."

"It wasn't my fish."

"What's that?"

"It wasn't my fish. I got it from the canal."

"Don't talk back, you understand?"

"Then why ask?"

"Eh?"

"Why ask if you don't want an answer?"

Tamai chuckles. His teeth shine in the darkness.

"Fuuuuuck. Lucky your dad's in a good mood today, or you'd get a belt in the face for being a smart-ass. Go on. Get out of here."

In his bedroom, Pajarito takes off his pants and sits on the edge of the bed holding them in one hand. He's so angry he clenches his teeth and tugs at the fabric until the stitches give way. The sound of the dry thread ripping pierces the night as it thickens outside the window.

One day he'll be grown and he'll beat the shit out of his dad, and anyone else with the nerve to tell him, like just then, outside the museum, that he's the same as Tamai. One day his body will be big enough for the fury he's lived with all his life.

After her foray to the Tamais', Estela got back into bed and held her husband tight. In his sleep, Miranda thought she wanted him and responded in kind, stroking her body under her flimsy nightgown, Estela's bare flesh that had settled with time: shapely still, though fuller than in her carnival queen days.

Trembling from what she'd just done, she let herself be led, answering Miranda's movements. He turned her onto her stomach and began tonguing her buttocks, drifting over the curve of them till he arrived down below.

Then she felt him climb on top of her, slide his hands under her chest, and grab hold of her tits. They both liked fucking this way. Him astride her, biting her neck, clutching her breasts like a horse's bridle. Her bucking her haunches, thrusting up and down so her husband's member could sink in all the way to the hilt, biting the pillow so she didn't cry out.

They loved each other and made a good pair.

Afterward, Miranda fell back onto the mattress and she nestled against his chest and felt calmer. She'd done the right thing in getting rid of the greyhound. Doubly so, because now her husband wouldn't suffer, and neither would the dog.

That's what she was thinking as she fell asleep. She'd done what she had to do, and after all, dead dogs don't bite.

Celina always stayed out of Tamai's business. That night, when Miranda left, she asked if he wasn't the man from the other brickworks. Tamai said yes. For a moment, she was cheered and thought maybe the guy had too much work—she knew he'd been in the brick trade for years—and had come to offer them some. But no, apparently he'd come about the dog. Wanting to buy it, her husband said.

The way things were going, with money so tight, Celina said he should have sold it.

"He wasn't offering much," said Tamai, "and this dog's not for sale. It's Sonia's."

"Don't be silly. A dog's another mouth to feed . . ."

"The dog stays, and that's final. Plus I wouldn't sell it to that jerk."

"Do you know him?"

"Well enough."

"Oh, you never said. Where from?"

"Around. Guy stuff, Celina, forget it. Give me Pajarito and go fix us something to eat."

She passed him the baby with a sigh.

"You might as well ask me to do magic tricks . . . There's nothing in the cupboard." She felt anxiety bubble up from the pit of her stomach. "I don't know what we're going to do."

"It'll be fine, woman. Here—you take the kid and I'll go to the store, maybe they'll give me something on credit."

Celina ran her hand over her eyes and picked up the baby. The boy gurgled and moved his arms, batting at a lock of his mother's hair. She smiled and held him tight.

"I'll take Sonia," Tamai said. "If I've got her with me, the guy at the store can hardly say no."

He lifted her up and Celina watched them leave. Father and daughter were chatting as they went: her babbling away in garbled sentences and him responding in a tender voice.

She hugged the baby to her chest again, so tight he whimpered and she quickly loosened her grip, afraid she'd hurt him. Even if Tamai managed to get some stuff on credit, her anxiety wasn't going anywhere.

For a while now she'd been thinking of visiting her father. Taking the kids along so he could meet them. Maybe with grandchildren paving the way, the old man would soften. Though she'd sworn never to see him again, not even on the day of his funeral, if things carried on like this she'd have to swallow her pride and see if he'd forgive her.

She left the baby in the crib on the patio, left him in nothing but a diaper so he could cool off a bit, and sat down to have a think. She looked at the starry sky and lit a cigarette from the pack her husband had forgotten on the table. She had a feeling she was pregnant again. The past few days she'd been dizzy and nauseated. Since she was still breastfeeding, she hadn't had her period, and sometimes she muddled up the days of the cycle; more than once, Tamai had forgotten to pull out. As soon as she noticed his mistake, Celina was equally annoyed with both of them, herself and her husband, for being so reckless, but what was done was done.

In those days screwing was the one pleasure they could afford;

fun, free-of-charge, shared moments of bliss that were hard to turn down. Their marriage wasn't going well and things were no better since Tamai became his own boss. Instead he worked half-heartedly and the few customers they found lost patience, and just as the brickmaker took his time about the work, they took their time about paying.

Sometimes Celina thought sex was all the love they had left. Only in bed could they feel close to each other and far away from their everyday woes.

They were both hot-blooded. Celina had known no other man than Tamai, but with him she became an experienced woman. He'd made her an addict and she couldn't sleep at night if he didn't satisfy her. Even when he came home drunk, she made sure he got hard enough for her to ride.

He'd never stand by and let her make peace with her family. But just as there were things he didn't share with her, she could do things behind his back. If her old man agreed to help her out, and Tamai ended up with a plate of food and a tumbler of wine on the table, Celina knew he wouldn't ask where it came from.

The Mirandas' finances weren't doing so great either. Elvio Miranda was a good brickmaker, maybe the best in town, shored up by his family history in the trade, but he was another man who liked to do things his way and didn't keep up with the work. He preferred training his racing dogs to shoveling soil all day long and carting it to the pisadero. Every so often he'd hire some young guy to help, but since he didn't keep up with the wages, either, the helpers all left in the end.

If they had enough to eat, it was only because Estela took charge of the household finances and started doing people's sewing.

When Estela was a teenager, Señora Nena, her godmother, sent her to study dressmaking, and though she hadn't made more than a couple of dresses—there was no need, she worked and her godmother never let her want for anything—she'd gone back to it later, helping with the costumes for the carnival dancers. She'd always been an enterprising woman, and though she let Miranda convince her to quit her job as a secretary when they married, on seeing the way things were going, she sent for the Singer from her unmarried days and put signs up in the local stores offering basic sewing services.

Señora Nena had told her that money worries could spoil even the best of marriages, and Estela, who had married for love and meant it to last, refused to let that happen to them. Elvio Miranda might have been useless, but she adored him, he was the father of her child and the man she hoped to grow old with: if he wasn't going to earn any money, she'd make sure they had at least enough to get by.

Without Miranda's addictions, which she indulged as if the man were a child, they'd have been better off: from alterations, hemming, and mending, Estela quickly moved on to making clothes, and soon she was sewing her first wedding dress. It wasn't that Miranda asked her for money or took any from her in secret, but rather that she, not wanting her husband to feel like less of a man, always slipped something into his pockets to tide him over.

Marciano lifts one arm—the effort is agony—and strokes his father's cheek, his stubble; he tries to reach his hair, which is longer than before, wavy and brown, but his arm falls back and hits the ground with a thud, like an old lady fainting at a funeral. He looks so young, his father. As if no time had passed.

"Dad, remember when we went hunting in Entre Ríos?"

Miranda laughs.

"'Course. In Antonio's pickup."

Marciano had loved it, it was like *The Adventures of Tom Sawyer*, the thick vegetation on either side of the river, the muggy heat, the insects. They'd taken a little motorboat and followed the water as it wound its way between the small islands.

He was eleven. The following year, in just a few months, in fact, his father would die. But at the time, his dad was full of life. Miranda had longer hair then and a longer beard, too, and the steam that came from the banks, or from the river itself, from the sun that beat down on the riverbed and warmed up the silt, the steam in the atmosphere, dampened his hair, stuck it to his head and face. He smiled and gazed into the distance. Antonio did too. The older men didn't speak and neither did Marciano. As if the landscape had left them breathless. All you could hear was the noise of the engine and the water the boat was slicing through.

Eventually they stopped and got out, wading through the

water, then Antonio and his father pulled the boat up the little sand beach and they made a fire. Night was beginning to fall, but where they were, with so many trees, it was already dark.

That evening they ate a rice stew. The men stayed up chatting till late, swapping stories from hunts gone by, their own and other people's, comparing notes on how to catch a capybara.

Marciano lay on a mat and listened for a while, wanting to learn, to memorize all the stories so he could boast to his friends, until the men's voices began to fade, merging with the rustling plants and the water, the squawks of nocturnal birds, the sound of a snapped twig now and then under an animal's feet.

"Remember when I said I wanted to go and live there?"

Miranda says nothing. He's gazing into the distance, like that time on the boat, but he doesn't smile.

"Remember, Dad?"

"Hmm?"

"Me wanting to go and live in Entre Ríos . . ."

"Oh, yeah, you going to? But you're not looking too well, son . . ."

"No, Dad."

He wanted to live in a place like that. With all that green, all that water; even the birds were more beautiful than here, with brighter feathers, more colorful beaks. Here everything's hard, dry, spiky, covered in dust. People were probably friendlier there, even. Here it's different, here all anyone knows is violence and force.

That morning, when Tamai found the dead greyhound, its eyes glazed over and its head resting in a puddle of drool and blood, he was so furious he kicked it in the ribs, as if that could get it back on its feet.

It had to be that sonofabitch Miranda.

He snatched the chain from the post and set off at a march, pulling the carcass behind him. Celina, who was just getting up, saw him and walked out to the patio.

"What happened?"

"That fucking piece of shit poisoned my dog."

"Who? What are you talking about?"

"Miranda, who else? He poisoned it or fed it ground glass, I don't know, it's all the same thing: the dog's dead."

"So where are you going?"

"To confront the bastard."

"Oh, don't. Just stay here. Let's bury it before Sonia gets up and sees."

Tamai ignored her and carried on. The greyhound's body, now slightly swollen, thudded along the dry, dusty ground. He dragged it the hundred yards to Miranda's place and pushed the gate open with his foot.

Estela's blood froze when she spotted him through the window. She came out right away to meet him.

"Where's Miranda, ma'am?"

"He's . . . he's not here . . . look . . ."

"I'd like a word with him."

"Listen . . . my husband's got nothing to do with this . . ."

Estela looked at the animal and her eyes filled with tears.

"Miranda! Get your ass outside! You hear me? Come out here!"

"Please, Tamai, don't shout, the baby's sleeping. I can explain . . . my husband has nothing to do with it."

"Get out here, you pussy! Or would you rather hide behind your wife?"

The commotion woke Miranda. He pulled on his pants and went out to see what was going on.

"What the hell?" he said.

He looked at Tamai, who raised his arm, shaking the thick chain, and then he saw it.

Now it was his eyes that were glistening. He ran over and knelt beside the dog.

"Poor thing, poor little guy . . . ," he managed to say, before Tamai booted him in the jaw and sent him tumbling back onto the cracked earth.

"You killed my dog, you sonofabitch."

Taking advantage of his enemy's confusion, Oscar Tamai lunged at Miranda. Miranda quickly regained his senses and they began to wrestle, rolling over the bumpy ground until they fell into the mud of the pisadero.

Estela followed them, shouting.

"Stop! It was me! It was me!"

But neither man would listen. They were like two fighting dogs. Miranda managed to shake Tamai off and clambered to his feet. The other man followed, crawling out of the pit that was slick with the mixture for making bricks. They were both gasping for breath, caked in mud; Tamai's yellow eyes glinted like the blades of twin knives, seeking his enemy's heart.

"This . . . isn't over," he said, his voice breaking with rage and exertion.

"I ought . . . to kill you," Miranda replied, hands on his knees, trying to draw air into his lungs.

"You wanted your fucking dog back . . . well, now you've got it," said Tamai, making for the gate.

When he passed by the body, he kicked it again, with the last of his strength, as if he wanted to send it flying. But the animal was heavy by now and hard as a rock.

Some neighbors who'd looked out when they heard all the yelling turned away and sipped their maté when they saw him coming past their houses; they weren't about to risk an earful for rubbernecking.

Estela, in tears, took her husband by the arm and led him onto the patio, where there was a tap and a sink for washing clothes. She connected a hose and doused him all over, scrubbing with one hand to get the mud off.

"He's lost it, he's fucking insane," said Miranda, lowering his head so his wife could wash his hair as well.

When he was presentable, Estela turned off the tap and went to the clothesline for a towel and handed it to him.

He dried his hair, which was dripping, and then hung the towel around his neck. With his pants and torso soaking wet, barefoot as he had been since getting out of bed, he strode over to where the greyhound's body had ended up. He looked down at it, hands on hips.

"Christ. Poor old fellow. It's a damn shame."

Estela went over and held him from behind.

"It was me, Miranda," she said.

He spun around like he'd been bitten by a snake.

"What did you say?"

"I killed it . . ."

The woman covered her face with her hands and sobbed.

"What are you saying, Estela?"

"Me. It was me . . . I couldn't keep watching you suffer over that animal."

Miranda shook his head and wiped his face with a corner of the towel.

"I'm sorry. I thought it would fix everything once and for all . . . I don't know what came over me . . . I wasn't thinking."

"Estela . . . you don't know Tamai."

Without another word, he crouched and removed the collar and chain, took the dog in his arms, and made for the yard, skirted some piles of bricks, and continued out to the edge of his property. He put the greyhound down on a patch of grass and stroked it, then shook his head again, aggrieved.

He retraced his steps, found a spade, went back to the yard, and started to dig.

Estela watched from a distance, she couldn't bring herself to get any closer.

It was scorching by now and her husband's hunched back gleamed in the sun, his foot coming down hard on the shovel as he dug out chunks of dirt and piled them on one side. When the hole was deep enough, he took the body by its four legs and threw it in. Then he replaced the dirt, flattened it out with the back of the shovel, and sat down and caught his breath. He rested one hand on the cool soil, as if laying it on the body of the greyhound.

When Celina saw Tamai approaching, she gasped and ran out to meet him.

"Sweet mother of god, what happened?"

He walked straight past without answering, went to a tap, filled a bucket with water, held it above his head with both arms, and poured it all over himself. Then he turned the tap on again to refill it. Suddenly, he burst out laughing.

Celina watched him, perplexed. He'd obviously had a run-in with the neighbor, but what was so funny?

"Go get the soap and sponge and give me a hand," he said, still chuckling.

Celina went in to get them, and when she returned to the patio, Tamai was naked, pouring more water over himself with the bucket. She helped him clean off the mud, soaping his hair until it was covered in grayish froth, and rinsing him with a jug of water. Then she brought a towel and started to dry him, patting him gently all over his body and giving his scalp a vigorous rub.

He'd sat down to make her job easier, and now he grabbed her around the waist and pulled her into his lap. She inspected the cut on his temple.

"I'll put something on that so it heals quicker."

He nodded and hugged her. Celina felt her eyes well up and rested her chin on her husband's shoulder.

Soon their third child would be born. She was so harried she'd not even thought about names or sorted out any clothes. Luckily there were a bunch left over from Pajarito: he'd grown so fast that some had barely been worn. But she still had to get them out of the box, wash them, give them an airing. Buy some cloth and make diapers. She held Tamai's body tighter. Sometimes she was scared he'd get killed. He was always picking fights with someone or other, and now with the neighbor too. It was hopeless. And what would she do then, as a widow with small children?

She dried her eyes with the back of her hand and stood up. He buried his face in her belly and stroked her backside.

"You need to give it a rest," she told him, running her fingers through his hair.

He looked up at her with those narrow yellow eyes and nodded, barely moving his head.

Now that he'd calmed down, his whole body was beginning to ache from the tussle with Miranda.

Listen, Pájaro, listen. Don't fall asleep on me, okay? Helloooo, I'm talking to you . . . Come on, Pájaro, wakey-wakey. Can you hear that? Can you? Can you hear it too? What is it? Some kind of moaning, right? Where's it coming from? Over there? From over there, you think? I dunno. Sounds nearer to me. A moan like a dry hinge. Oh, no, of course, it's the seats swinging. Were you scared? What did you think it was, man, a ghost? It's just there's a bit of a breeze now, can you feel it?

You know a ton about these rides. One summer you got it into your head to run away with a fair like this one. How old would you have been? Twelve, thirteen? You used to come and talk to the staff. Some wouldn't give you the time of day. But others stopped to explain how the rides worked, and even let you help tighten the screws or grease the parts. Everything needs to be oiled just right so nothing squeaks and scares the public. You asked them questions about life with the fair. What it was like moving from place to place, on the road, with nothing tying you down. Whether they missed their families. Trying to figure out if you were brave enough to join them.

One time you just up and left. You were tiny then. Five or six. Your dad had given you a thrashing for something—or for nothing. You put three oranges in a bag and took them with you, down the old road to Santa Ana. You'd gotten pretty far when the sun started to set. You stopped and ate all three oranges, one after another. The bushes by the roadside were darkening and looked taller than before. A noise startled you. It was some loose horses, munching on tree leaves. Seeing them suddenly, all three black or seeming black from a distance, they were like three hooded men. You carried on. When the truck appeared up ahead, you didn't even think about hiding. It would've been easy: just drop to your belly in the ditch. But no, you kept walking to meet it. The man braked. The sky was on fire.

"What are you doing out here by yourself?" he asked.

You didn't answer.

"Aren't you Tamai's boy? Hop in, I'll give you a ride."

You did as you were told.

No one found out about your attempted escape. You were mad that not even your mom realized you were gone. Good thing your father didn't notice, though, or you'd have caught it twice as bad.

That night, in bed with your belly full, you were still angry, even if deep down you were also glad.

But fuck, those empty seats are creaking like hell. When the ride's full and the music's playing, you don't notice.

Marciano used to sit outside on nights when the heat made it impossible to stay indoors. Almost every night of the year, that is, except in winter, which was brief as a sigh. The whole neighborhood always stayed outdoors till late, till their tiredness got the better of the heat, till their bodies gave in and grew resigned to the torpid rooms with fans that sent hot air over their sweaty skin, barely moving the smoke from the mosquito coils.

As a boy, he'd been in the street with the others. Running, jumping, riding a bike seemed to keep them cooler than sitting still. They caught the moths off the streetlamps or strayed into the darkness of the empty lots, chasing fire beetles. They trapped them in glass jars and put them on their bedside tables and fell asleep listening to the tac-tac the insects made when they lit their tiny lanterns.

As a teenager, he'd meet up with the guys on some street corner to smoke, drink beer, and joke around with the girls, who were always in groups of two or three, strutting around nearby. All the guys barefoot, naked but for shorts, showing off their sinewy bodies, the emerging pecs and biceps that hard physical labor was beginning to shape.

Sometimes he stayed home till someone came and talked him into playing the arcade games in town. He'd sit in a deck chair, with the swanky boom box he bought himself each year, which got bigger each time, with more lights and knobs and switches, and ever more powerful speakers. He listened to Santa Fe cumbia and cuarteto, music he got from the DJ at the club, who was a friend of his. He smoked and drank beer and went on pondering the idea of moving to Entre Ríos.

He remembered the time he went with his father, the only trip they got to go on together and the only trip he'd taken anywhere. He closed his eyes and saw the river again, the trees, the grassy hillsides; again his cheeks felt the cool air rising from the water, the breeze sweetly poisoned by the scent of the flowers that grew on the banks.

He didn't know the name of the place they'd spent those days with Antonio. It didn't matter. It was Entre Ríos, and Entre Ríos was surely all the same, watery and green.

At those times, he got wistful and sad and cranked the music right up so his mom and siblings wouldn't guess how he was feeling.

Then he told himself that before going off to Entre Ríos, he had to avenge his father's death. It was years ago and they'd closed the case after just a few months, but he couldn't forget, he carried it with him every day of his life.

After the fight with Miranda, Tamai thought he'd better let things cool off, at least for a bit. They'd been due a proper reckoning ever since that distant night in the bar when the guys had held them back. Their fists had clearly been thirsting for it and that morning had slaked the craving.

Miranda was a good fighter, he'd give him that. Tamai had been sore down to his bones for days. And besides, the way the whole thing played out was fair enough: he'd stolen a racing dog and ruined it, then the other guy had killed it. Deep down, he didn't care about the animal's death, he knew it hurt Miranda more than him. But he'd gotten his revenge, and that was how it should be.

He hadn't liked the way Celina looked at him when she told him to give it a rest. Although they didn't always get along and he felt like a prisoner in the brickworks and he'd even thought about throwing in the towel and moving away, the fact was that for the first time ever he had something in his life, he had a family—he, who'd grown up an orphan, who'd never stuck around anywhere long, had a family, and a real man has to look after his family.

So he decided to clean up his act. He was twenty-seven by then and their third child was on the way. Celina was a good woman and the worst thing for him would be if she decided to go back to her father. If she left him, that old bastard would have won. And Tamai wasn't the losing type.

Remembering his old grudge against his father-in-law dampened his anger at Miranda. He'd show that old man and his spinster daughters that Oscar Tamai was worth more than all three of them put together.

For the first time he felt like a new man, the kind of guy who was able to get his life on track, who was able to do things right. And he'd worked it out for himself, he hadn't needed some priest or government mencho to tell him. His own wits had shown him the way.

The years of Tamai's conversion were the happiest ones for Celina and the children. It wasn't more than three and they went by in a flash: like all good things, you start getting comfortable, then bam.

But they managed to do a lot. Tamai proved he could be not just his own boss but also his best employee. He got up at dawn and worked all through the day, breaking only for lunch and a siesta. He gave up seeing his drinking buddies. He didn't give up drinking, but he drank his wine quietly, at home, with his family. Very soon after the third baby came, Celina got herself a fourth.

And during that time, Leyes, the owner of the brickworks, came back, wanting to sell because he'd settled down south ("I'm done with this hellhole now that my old mom's passed," he said), and they bought the place thanks to what they'd saved and Leyes's haste to be done with it all and get back to his job on the oil rig.

Celina was pleased. Raising the children and looking after the house kept her busy, and she'd stopped thinking of going back to her father. She was glad she'd stuck it out and waited a little longer.

She had no idea what was behind this radical change in Tamai, and wasn't going to dig too deep to find out. The reasons didn't matter, what mattered was that every day her husband grew more like the husband she'd always wanted.

Now if she thought about her father and sisters, it was with renewed bitterness: she wished they could see her, happy and surrounded by children, with a man who was working his fingers to the bone so she and the little ones had everything they needed. But as soon as she thought of them like that, she stopped. Celina was fearful and suspected those thoughts might come back to haunt her.

Elvio Miranda's murder was big news and even made the regional paper.

Deaths in bar fights between drunks, like so-called crimes of passion, were so common they were rarely mentioned, even on the radio. No one, not the police, journalists, or regular people, paid much attention unless they knew the victim or the suspect.

However, the grisly nature of this murder—two bullets and a slit throat—plus the fact that Miranda was from a well-known family, meant it caused more of a stir.

Rebolledo, one of the policemen who'd gone to tell Estela the news, had been in her class in grade school. Estela sewed clothes for the police commissioner's wife. And everyone remembered her as the longtime carnival queen: she might have gained weight and aged a little, but her smile could always dust things with the glitter of those nights full of dancing, streamers, and sequins.

Because of all this, the case was taken fairly seriously, and there was even an investigation.

They never found a culprit. Miranda wasn't exactly squeaky-clean: on top of his gambling debts, there'd been no shortage of disputes with customers of the brickworks and the owners of racing dogs.

The greyhound scene was underground, and the breeders and trainers had a sketchy reputation. So did the construction firms who bought the bulk of Miranda's bricks: people who cut deals with the provincial government, big fish who could easily kill a guy, or have him killed, more likely, and then carry on with their lives.

On top of the other minor enemies he'd made from scuffles in bars, there was the old feud with his neighbor Oscar Tamai, another brickmaker: the whole neighborhood knew about their constant fights and they'd all heard them threatening to kill each other.

No doubt about it: so many suspects meant none at all.

They went through the motions all the same, taking statements from the patrons at the Imperio who were the last people to see him alive, and calling in his potential enemies—without troubling the construction firm owners, of course. First they'd do a general sweep, and then, if they had to go back with a fine-tooth comb, they'd see.

The police station hadn't been so busy in ages: people were in and out all day long, the cops' fingers blunted from bashing the typewriter keys and their backs shot from hunching over the machine.

In a way this was all good practice for what happened a couple of months later, burying the investigation into the brickmaker's murder for good: the robbery of the provincial bank.

An event straight out of a movie, which was the talk of the town for months to come and would remain, over the years, one of those after-dinner stories wheeled out from time to time, always with some extra embellishment.

The summons came for Oscar Tamai one afternoon, brought by a very young policeman on a bicycle. He was expected in two days' time.

On the given date Tamai strolled into the police station, cool as a cucumber. Freshly shaved, with his clothes pressed and his boots polished. It was a sweltering day and the police officers' uniforms had dark stains at the chest and armpits. The glass ashtrays were overflowing and everyone looked wiped out.

"Have a seat, Tamai," said one officer.

The interviewee sat down in a chair facing the desk. He drew a pack of cigarettes from his shirt pocket and gestured to ask if he could light up. Just to play ball, really, since the smoke in the air made it pretty obvious.

Officer Rebolledo nodded and took a cigarette when Tamai held out the pack. Tamai repeated his offer to the others and they all accepted.

He lit his cigarette and leaned back in his chair, waiting for the questioning to start. But the cops were tired of the whole thing. For a moment they all stared at him as if they didn't know what the hell he was doing there.

"Should I make some tereré?" the same baby-faced cop who'd brought him the summons asked Rebolledo.

"Go on, then. Maybe it'll wake us up a bit. We haven't slept a wink with all this mess," he said, turning to Tamai.

"So you have no idea who it was?"

Rebolledo snorted with laughter.

"Going by the statements, it could have been anyone. All I know for sure is it wasn't me. Or Mamani here, because he was with me"—and he pointed at another of the officers, laughing again.

He drank from the maté gourd the baby-faced police officer passed him, sucking till the metal straw made a noise. When he handed it back, the kid added more water, glanced at him, and then motioned to Tamai, asking permission to offer some to him. Rebolledo waved his arm in response, as if to say: "Be my guest, son."

Tamai took the maté. It was cold with a dash of lemon, delicious, and just what he needed on that blazing hot morning.

"Right," said Rebolledo. "Let's get started or we'll be here all day."

He took a blank sheet of paper from a stack on the desk and slotted it into the typewriter, then straightened it, fixed it in place, and began to take his statement.

The morning after Miranda's murder, the neighborhood was abuzz. When Celina got up and went onto the patio, her neighbor came straight over to the fence, as if he'd been waiting for her to wake up so he could be the first to tell her the news.

"You heard what's happened, Celina?"

"No. Here I am, barely out of bed, and already you're bringing me gossip," she said, smiling.

"I wish it was just gossip, ma'am."

The guy took a sip of maté. Celina frowned.

"Why? What's happened?"

"Something awful."

Celina looked around, and, yes, the neighborhood did seem different. Women huddled together talking in the street and on the sidewalk. Lots of comings and goings.

"What . . ."

"It's Elvio Miranda. He's been killed like a dog."

Her blood froze and instinctively she glanced back at her house, at the room where her husband was still sleeping.

"I can't believe it," she said.

"It's true. Sad to say, but it's true. That poor wife of his, such a lovely woman."

"But how did it happen? When?"

"Last night. Seems some folks waited in the street for him,

shot him a few times, and then—" And the man, without finishing his sentence, ran his index finger horizontally across his throat.

Now Celina felt her stomach turn over. She leaned against a tree.

"Are you feeling okay?" the neighbor asked, putting down his gourd and starting to step over the wire fence.

"Yes . . . it's just . . . it's such horrible news. I feel a bit light-headed. I'm fine . . . Maybe I'll go lie down."

"Poor thing. Have a spoonful of sugar, ma'am, that'll put some color in your cheeks."

"I will. It's fine. Thanks."

Celina walked slowly toward her house, unsteady on her feet. Her neighbor's murder was horrifying, but more horrifying still was the dreadful thought that had crossed her mind.

She went into their bedroom, which was dark, the air thick with the scent of sleeping bodies. She really did feel light-headed, so she gingerly lay down on the bed, not wanting to wake her husband quite yet. She had to think hard about what she was going to say to him. She'd need to tread very carefully if she wanted him to tell her the whole truth.

With her gaze fixed on the ceiling, she tried to run through the events of the night before.

Tamai had left after dinner like he always did, on the bicycle. She'd cleaned the kitchen and then sat outside, Sonia helped bring the TV out, and the two of them watched the telenovela together and then the news. Pajarito went off to the arcades with his friends, and the little ones were playing in the street. When the programming was over, she sent Sonia to get her siblings and put them all to bed. She left them a mosquito coil and arranged the fan so they all got a bit of air.

Then she went back to the patio and sat down to flick through a magazine a neighbor had lent her. She smoked a cigarette. After an hour or so, Pajarito came home and they went to bed.

It took her a while to get to sleep, because of the heat. But eventually she dropped off and didn't even feel her husband getting into bed beside her. She slept right through till morning, and had no idea what time Tamai had come back, or in what state.

She lit the lamp on her side of the bed and watched the man, who was sleeping deeply. She leaned over and sniffed. He smelled faintly of alcohol, but no more than usual. Getting up, she looked for the clothes he'd taken off and left on the floor at the foot of the bed. She held them up to the light and inspected them thoroughly. Nothing seemed different about them.

She put the clothes down and sat on the edge of the bed and turned out the light. In the darkness, her heart flipped over again: Did she really think Tamai was capable of killing someone?

Marciano got his first baby sibling when he was five. Estela, remembering the old nurse who'd looked after her the last time she gave birth, called him Ángel, and, true to his name, the boy hardly made a sound. More than once, his mother even got up from the sewing machine and bent over his crib to make sure he was still breathing.

She liked how her children were so different, despite both being boys. Marciano had cried all the time and never settled, and this one really was a little angel.

As for Marciano, he wasn't sure how he felt about the new arrival. Before, he thought he was missing out by not having brothers or sisters, because all the other kids had at least one. He was an only child and felt a bit jealous that they always had someone to play with or even fight with, while he had to sit around waiting for a game or fight to come his way.

When the baby was inside his mother's belly, Marciano was fine with it: they didn't know if it was a girl or a boy, and although his mother wanted a little girl, he was secretly rooting for a boy so they'd have more in common and he could pass on all the stuff he was learning. He had friends with older brothers and they always spoke of them admiringly, as if simply being born first made them more important.

But now and then he was gripped by something he couldn't explain, and he thought that when the baby was born, he himself was going to die. At those times, he took out all his soldiers, Indians, model cars, all the toys he had, lined them up on the patio, and then lay on his tummy and looked at them one by one, as if bidding them farewell.

It wasn't till the day he and his dad went to the hospital to meet his little brother that Marciano realized it wouldn't be just him in the house anymore, and that he didn't like that.

He squeezed his dad's hand tighter as they went under the arched entrance to the old building and through the gravel court-yard. Even tighter when they stepped inside and he smelled the medical smell and saw the tiled walls. Tighter still as they made their way down the corridor past rooms with open doors, hearing the sounds of coughing and wheezing, a child crying, an old man's groans. And he buried his nails in his dad's flesh when they glimpsed the first nurse. At that point Miranda decided to pick him up, and Marciano clasped him so tightly around the neck he almost strangled him.

He was terrified of the hospital. All the other times they'd been there, it had never been for anything good: medication, vaccinations, shots, and even a cast on his arm after a fall the previous year. The memory of the broken bone was still fresh. If this was where his brother was coming from, surely it didn't bode well.

His parents thought that eventually Marciano would get over being jealous of his brother. But his emotions were all over the place: sometimes he felt an irrepressible love for the newborn, and other times an equally irrepressible desire to smash him against the floor. Sometimes he wanted him to grow up so he could take him to the canal to go fishing, and other times he wanted him to grow up so he could take him to the canal and drown him.

A year and a half after Angelito, Estela had the twins, and then, full house, decided to get her tubes tied.

The arrival of their twin sisters slightly improved things for Marciano and Ángel. Or for Marciano, really, since Ángel was little still and all he felt for his brother was unconditional love.

At his age, seven, Marciano thought girls were the absolute worst, so he saw the use in having a brother around: holding their own, two against two, not outnumbered.

Still, they never saw eye to eye. Marciano loved Angelito, but he adopted a distant and severe attitude toward him, as if he were never satisfied, as if he always expected more from the kid. And Angelito spent all his time trying to please his older brother but wound up puzzled by his reactions.

With Miranda's death, the distance between them grew. Marciano felt he had to take his father's place, and his natural severity toward his brother intensified: as if it were on him, a boy of just twelve, that the other's future depended.

Three hours after going into the office where they took his statement, Tamai was back in the dusty street and the scorching midday sun. He lit a cigarette, and as he walked, he sought the squat shade of the pata de buey trees that grew on the sidewalk. Their branches were laden with white flowers.

The death of his longtime rival had thrown him. He'd never imagined things ending that way. The other man's death made his own feel more real, and now it seemed more likely to be violent.

Although they'd threatened each other countless times, he'd never have had it in him to murder Miranda, and he didn't think his neighbor could have killed him, either.

Maybe once or twice, blinded by hatred, he'd thought about seeing him dead. But now that it had happened, it felt like a low blow. Fate stepping in to screw him over, even if it was the other man who'd died.

His old quarrel with Miranda was an affirmation of himself. And all the dirty tricks they played on each other had kept things interesting. What was he supposed to do now that he'd been left alone?

Acting on the neighbors' statements, the police put Tamai on the suspect list, though more as a formality than out of genuine conviction. Faced with Rebolledo's tired, bloodshot eyes and the other officers' yawns, he had to go through all the times he and

Miranda had quarreled. Or almost all: there were so many they blurred together.

The tongue-wagging neighbors had described each incident in detail, and when Tamai hesitated, when his thoughts formed a kind of cloud, Rebolledo or one of his assistants would look through the papers and prompt him.

"How about the time Miranda stole a goat from you? Before Christmas one year, it says here."

The goat! That motherfucker! Tamai clapped a hand to his forehead and laughed. Miranda, the swine, had waited until he'd killed and skinned the goat, until he'd marinated it, if he remembered right. He'd gone out to buy wood to make the fire, and when he came home, pretty late, admittedly, since he'd stopped by a bar on the way, the patio table where he'd left the animal ready for the grill was bare. From the other end of the block came the mouthwatering smell of roasting meat. Yep, just before Christmas. Celina had taken the kids to the nativity play and there was no one at home and his neighbor had seized his chance.

He'd marched straight to the sidewalk outside Miranda's place.

"Goddamn sonofabitch," he'd yelled.

The other guy, lit by the flames, had raised his glass and replied: "Merry Christmas, neighbor."

"Did you threaten him then?"

"'Course I did . . . Thanks to him I had to run out for some fucking chicken before my wife got home."

"It says here you once tried to set fire to Miranda's house . . ."

"No, sir, it wasn't like that. No way."

"What was it like, then?"

"It was an accident."

One time, he'd been on his way home in the early hours, pretty far gone. He passed his neighbor's place and happened to notice the guy had been firing bricks. You could still see a few live embers. And the thing was, that summer there'd been a terrible drought. Miranda had a few square feet of dry grass in his backyard, and Tamai decided to give him a scare and set fire to it. Then when it was alight, he'd sound the alarm and watch from the street as the guy came racing out in his underwear to stop the blaze. It'd be hilarious.

And that's just what he did. But it turned out Miranda wasn't home, he was playing Mus at the Imperio or somewhere, and his wife almost had a heart attack and called the firefighters. It wasn't serious. Maybe he'd even done him a favor by clearing the yard of overgrown grass, which would've been full of snakes. But some tattletale saw him and said he'd tried to burn the house down. Which was bullshit.

"The next day, it says here, you and Miranda came to blows in the street and everyone heard you threatening each other. 'I'm going to slit your throat,' this statement has you saying."

Tamai shook his head.

"Things you say in the heat of the moment, officer. Doesn't the statement have what he said to me?"

"That's beside the point, Tamai, because he's the one who's dead."

Tamai clucked his tongue. "Well, when you put it like that . . . ," he muttered.

"And it says here you had a fight at a dog race . . . and another at the hunting and fishing club on Workers' Day, six years back . . . a fight with broken bottles at a carnival dance . . . you stole a thousand bricks from him and sold them as your own, according to someone else . . . then there was a fistfight at a kids' soccer match at School 11 . . . at the Imperio . . . at the Titop nightclub . . ." Rebolledo leafed through page after page and with each one the list grew longer. He sighed and ran a hand over his sweaty face. "You two never saw eye to eye, buddy."

"Maybe not. But I didn't kill him."

The officer leaned back in his faux leather chair, which creaked under his weight, and clasped his hands over his belly.

"Where were you that night?"

"At La Boyita, the pool hall on the way out of town. I was there till five that morning. A pal gave me a ride home in his car because I was a bit worse for wear. You can ask. There were a few of us . . . someone's sure to remember."

When Tamai left the police station, Rebolledo stood up, pressed his palms to his lower back, and stretched, cracking his spine. The others had gone to get some food, and only he and the rookie were left.

Rebolledo went to a window overlooking a cement courtyard. Some geraniums, black from the blistering sun, wilted in the brick flower beds. The sight depressed him. Nélida, the old lady who answered the phone and cleaned the police station once a week, could start tending that little garden, he thought. It wouldn't take much work, certainly less than hanging around on the sidewalk nattering away about the station's goings-on. A few plants wouldn't be too much to ask, a bit of green, something nice to look at through the window.

He shook his head.

"Think it was him, sir?"

The young cop's wavering voice made him jump.

"Hmm?"

"D'you think Tamai killed Miranda?"

"Nah. I doubt it . . ."

"But based on the statements they were always at each other's throats . . ."

Rebolledo shrugged.

"Gossip. I'm not saying it's not true what people said, and it's all there in the records. Besides, Tamai didn't deny that stuff. But

I don't think it was him. I know him, we've had him in a bunch of times for making a scene. But he didn't do it. Tamai may be a no-good indio, but he wouldn't kill anyone like that. If you told me it was a bar fight, a stabbing, someplace public, I'd believe you. But the way Miranda was killed, no sir. Not a chance."

He went over to the floor fan they were using to boost the one on the ceiling, set it not to move, and held his face to the blades.

"Go across the street and get yourself a Coke. Then take the list of names Tamai gave us and call them in this afternoon. Especially the owner of La Boyita and the friend he said dropped him off that night."

The young cop nodded a few times and strode out. Rebolledo closed his eyes and the current of air slowly dried his damp face.

Poor Estela, he thought. They'd known each other since they were kids, they were in the same class through fifth grade, then he'd had to repeat the year and fell behind. He'd even tried to make a move on her back in the day, but then, who hadn't? She was the prettiest of all the girls, and the nicest . . . but she never gave him a chance, always feeding him that line about being friends and knowing each other since they were this high and him being like a cousin to her . . . those lies women come out with when they want nothing to do with you.

Maybe he wasn't the greatest catch, but Estela had tons of other offers: young guys, old guys, even cotton gin engineers and gringo landowners had tried their luck. And she still went and ended up with Miranda. Elvio had always been a looker and a ladies' man, but even so, throwing her lot in with Elvio Miranda of all people . . . and see where it got her, poor Estela, a widow and the kids still so little.

Pajarito can feel the shutters coming down. He's struggling to breathe, taking tiny gulps of air, as if he's in a sealed room and needs to ration what little oxygen is left. He blinks a few times and tries to stay awake. Moving his eyes first one way, then the other, in case that perks him up.

Fuck's sake, isn't anyone coming? Have they forgotten all about him, the assholes?

His nostrils quiver; he desperately wants to scream but knows his body won't let him.

"Watch the gun!"

He's twelve years old and has one toy pistol in each hand. He and his friends are playing on some empty land near the house: they're pretending to rob the provincial bank. If they don't let him be the gunman, Pajarito won't play. And since the guns are his, no one can say no.

They've stacked some fruit crates as a makeshift counter. Behind it, two kids count pieces of paper as if they're money. To one side, some cardboard boxes form the security guard's booth. A few littler kids are the customers. When the stage is set, Pajarito and his henchmen burst in from the street, running and shouting. He comes first and pretends to kick open the glass doors of the bank. He has one gun in each hand and he aims left and right, yelling for everyone to get down. His two accomplices, each with a piece of wood instead of a gun, make for the counter with plastic bags for the cash. Then what do you know, an absent-minded customer wanders into the bank. Pajarito reacts explosively, wheeling around and firing several shots near his feet.

"Watch the gun! Watch the gun!" the others yell at the new arrival, who proceeds to faint from the shock.

When they've stuffed the bags full of cash, they go back into the street. They move fast, but already the police are pulling up. This is Pájaro's moment, and as he runs backward to the car waiting on the corner, he shoots at the police again and again, shooting both guns at once, just like in the movies.

He smiles, his head ringing again with the gun sounds they made with their mouths. From there the three of them would run and hide on a hill behind the neighborhood and the kids playing the police would chase them: the game could go on for hours until they were finally captured.

The robbery of the provincial bank had happened exactly like that. Playing at robbing the bank was the craze that whole year, and everyone wanted to be the shit-hot thief who could shoot two guns at the same time.

It all seems so far away now.

The first time he picked up a real gun, he realized how heavy they were and remembered the bank robber, and all his boyish admiration came back, because you'd need some serious skills even to hold a gun in each hand, up in the air, let alone to hit your mark.

He was never really into guns. He'd always preferred knives, light and precise. If one day he had to kill someone, he wanted it to be hand to hand.

A knife is almost like a continuation of your arm: you'd feel the other man's life slipping out through the wound, the enemy blood gushing up to the handle and wetting your clenched fist.

Now he knows. Now he knows what it's like on both sides: stabbing and being stabbed.

"Dad..."

Marciano feels something beginning to fade inside him.

"Dad, don't leave me . . . ," he stammers with tears in his eyes.

His father's still there, sitting in the mud, holding Marciano's head in his lap. But he's not looking at him. He's looking into the distance again, just like before, when Marciano was talking about Entre Ríos. Like when they were in the boat with Antonio, though his father's expression isn't blissful like it was back then. Now his expression is somber.

"Dad . . ."

He takes no notice, like he's a long way away or has other stuff on his mind.

"Dad!" he shouts and feels vomit rising at the back of his throat, the sour taste of all the beers he drank that night.

Then Miranda lowers his head and his bearded chin hides the scar. He looks at him, but his eyes are frightened.

"I let you down, Dad. I never found them. I never got my hands on them."

His father looks at him and frowns. He looks at him, cocking his head, as if surprised by the situation.

"Sh," he says. "Don't talk. You're in a bad way, kid. It's a damn shame," he says, averting his eyes.

Then he looks at him again and pats him a few times on the cheek.

"What's your name, kiddo?"

"I'm your son, Dad. I'm Marciano."

Miranda smiles.

"No . . . That's impossible, kid. How could you be my son, my son's a little boy. He'll be tucked in bed by now, at home, with his mom. Anyway, I should be getting back myself. My wife's a good woman, but she's got a temper. She's a handful if you cross her. And if I don't go now, she'll make me sleep outside."

"Don't leave me."

The man seems thoughtful. It's like something is fading inside him as well. He looks to one side, then the other. Lifts his eyes to the white sky, runs a hand over his face.

"Listen, kid. Listen carefully to what I'm about to say. I don't want to move you from here. You're injured and for all I know I'd make it worse. You keep calm, stay nice and still. I'll go and get help. My sticking around here won't fix anything."

"Don't go."

"Shush, now. Don't worry. Stay put. I won't leave you hanging, okay?"

He places his head carefully on the ground. Marciano can feel the damp through his hair. He watches his father get to his feet, though his upper body is still bent over him.

"You keep calm. I won't be long, kid, I won't be long."

"Don't go, Dad. Don't leave me alone."

After burying Miranda, Estela went home with her children. Señora Nena tried to persuade them to spend a few more days with her, for company and a change of scenery, but she said no. Sooner or later they'd have to go back because that was their house, the house they'd lived in with Miranda all those years. And not only the house, the brickworks. They couldn't just wash their hands of everything and start life over.

Life would keep going forever without Elvio Miranda, her loving husband and the father of her children. And she had to figure out how it would work.

So after the cemetery, she thought it best to go home. Miranda was dead and they all had to accept it and get on with their lives, and they might as well start right away.

Señora Nena would have rather they stayed with her awhile, or even moved in with her for good. She had a big empty house and was aging more quickly than she'd thought. But she knew Estela, she'd practically raised her, and she knew that when her mind was made up, there was nothing you could do.

So once they'd thrown a few handfuls of dry earth onto the casket and tossed some bougainvillea flowers into the grave, Estela took her children's hands and made them step back a little so the gravediggers could get to work. They stayed until the hole was completely full of earth and the grave had become a mound. The same workers put up a temporary wooden cross. During the week, the widow would set about choosing the tombstone, the decoration, some kind of plaque. For the time being, she and the little ones arranged the wreaths and bouquets people had brought.

After leaving Miranda sheltered by the shade of the palm leaves and ferns and purple spider plants that made up the floral arrangements, Estela took her children's hands again and the five of them walked down the narrow little path to the exit, where Señora Nena and some friends and relatives were waiting.

They said hello, and thank you, and got into their godmother's car, and she drove them home.

"Sure you don't want to come back to my place, dear?"

"I'm sure, Godmother."

With her hands on the steering wheel, Señora Nena nodded, understanding.

"All right, then. But you'll always be welcome, okay?"

Estela gave her a hug and felt her eyes welling up. She didn't want to crack. She had to stay whole to look after her children. Later, in bed by herself, she could cry in peace.

"Thank you, Godmother. Bye now. Coming, kids?"

She got out and opened the passenger door and helped them from the car. When they were all on the sidewalk, their godmother pulled away, vanishing in a cloud of dust.

"I wanted to go with Señora Nena," said one of the twins. "It's so nice at her house. Why can't we go and live there?"

"Because this is our house."

"But, Mommy, she has air-conditioning in every room and here it's always boiling."

Estela opened the gate and stepped aside to let the kids through. The twins went in sulkily, dragging their feet, as if hoping their mother would change her mind. Ángel, following his sisters, gave them a push to hurry them up. Marciano came last. His fists and teeth were clenched. It broke Estela's heart to see him so angry and forlorn, and still so young. Why did he have to go through all this?

Night was falling. They changed out of their dress clothes and into lighter, comfier things. Estela made cold chocolate milk for the kids and maté for herself and they all sat around the patio table.

It had been some years since they'd bought that long carob-wood table with its six chairs and set it up under the awning. Because of the heat that lasted most of the year, all the families' lives took place more on the patios than indoors.

As she drank her maté, Estela couldn't help staring at the empty chair at the table. Although really that chair had often been empty because Miranda hadn't spent much time at home. Only at lunch were they all together. As soon as the sun set, he showered, got changed, and headed into town to catch up with the guys, his drinking and gambling buddies.

But this was different. The chair would never have Miranda in it again.

Marciano, stirring his milk with a spoon but not drinking it, followed his mother's gaze. He, too, had been sneaking glances at the chair, unable to look at it directly. He would never see his dad again.

The twins and Angelito started arguing about the name of someone on TV. He was called this, no he wasn't, yes he was, that wasn't him, that was someone else, I swear.

Estela let them. Better they bicker than feel sad. But Marciano was livid and hurled his glass of milk at a tree. He'd been aiming at his siblings, to make them shut up, but he threw it too high and it sailed over their heads, not spilling until it shattered against the trunk in an explosion of liquid and broken glass.

"Shut up, you morons!" he yelled and got to his feet and glared at them, breathing hard, then ran away.

The twins burst into tears.

"What's wrong with my brother, Mom? Is he going to die too?" Angelito asked, trying hard not to join in his sisters' chorus of wails.

"No, darling . . . Don't say that. Leave him be, the poor thing. It'll pass."

Celina didn't dare go to Miranda's vigil. She wished she'd been brave enough: she felt sad about what had happened, and couldn't shake the thought that the dead man could have been her husband and she could've been the poor woman now raising her children alone.

Although she and Estela had never been part of the bad blood between Miranda and Tamai, had never really gotten involved, the fact was that each secretly blamed the other's husband for the feud that kept them permanently at odds.

Sometimes they ran into each other in a neighborhood shop or in meetings at school, since Pajarito and Marciano were in the same grade, but they never spoke, and each acted like the other didn't exist.

They were both well-mannered and would never have come to blows, though that wasn't unheard-of in the neighborhood: two women pulling each other's hair out in the street because of trouble with their husbands or children. They wouldn't even have gone as far as trading insults, something common enough among the other women living nearby.

Every now and then, separately, they'd each thought about talking it out, seeing if the two of them couldn't patch things up between their husbands. But then they'd quickly dismiss the idea: Who knew what Miranda and Tamai would do if they found out their wives were plotting to reconcile them?

The women didn't care so much if the men fought, but they

didn't like them dragging the whole family into it. Not that they did so directly: neither man ever had a hostile word or gesture for the other's wife or children, but one way or another, everyone was affected.

The morning Celina heard about her neighbor's death, she sat for a long time on the edge of the bed, unsure whether to wake her husband.

Tamai was lying on his back, snoring, dead to the world, moving only to slap the odd fly away from his face.

If he'd done something bad, he wouldn't be sleeping so soundly, Celina reassured herself. She wondered how best to tell him about Miranda so she could draw her own conclusions.

Maybe she should wake him up, send him off for a shower, brew him some maté, make sure he was fully alert, and only then tell him the bad news and see how he took it.

Or maybe not. Maybe it was better not to give him time, to take him by surprise, spring the story on him all at once and watch his reaction.

She was so lost in thought, pondering the right thing to do, that it made her jump when Tamai took her by the shoulders and began covering her neck with kisses. She hadn't realized he was awake.

Her husband licked her ear and undid her dress, which buttoned down the front. He fondled her tits with one hand and reached the other between her legs, to the slit that opened, moist and warm. Tamai swung his legs off the bed and sat her in his lap, took off her dress, and, as he moved his fingers inside her pussy, leaned her forward so he could tug on her nipples with his fingers, first one, then the other, as if milking her. And his taut tongue traveled down the crease of her ass.

When Celina began to tremble, he took her by the hips and

pulled her down hard on his stiff cock. Now, with both hands free, he kneaded her tits, squeezed them together in front of her, the nipples touching, rubbing, and then pulled them apart and stuck his head under her armpit to reach them with his tongue.

Celina, meanwhile, jiggled up and down in time with his thrusts.

Once they finished, she went to get a towel and wiped between her legs. Then she lay next to Tamai and used the same towel to clean the cum from his furry pelt. He stroked her hair and half closed his eyes, ready to sink back into the sleep of the dead.

But Celina shook him and made him open them and look at her.

"Was it you who killed Miranda?" she asked.

The second night without Miranda was the first one at home, in the bed they'd shared for more than twelve years. She'd spent the previous night at the vigil. Because of the circumstances of his death, and even with the legal paperwork involved in a murder case reduced, thanks to the efforts of Rebolledo and the police commissioner, they'd released the body only in the late afternoon. The vigil had lasted from that evening until the next afternoon, when he was buried.

By the time she put on her nightgown and got into bed, Estela hadn't closed her eyes for almost two days. The police had woken her in the early hours to tell her the bad news and she'd been on her feet ever since. The kids had slept a few hours in the funeral home: the twins on a sofa, and Ángel on two chairs they pushed together to form a bed. Marciano hadn't wanted to, but eventually exhaustion got the better of him as well and he dozed off where he sat.

Her godmother and the other women—neighbors, relatives—who'd been with her since they brought over the body tried to persuade her to go and lie down, or even to let them take her home, but Estela wouldn't hear of it. Not even at gunpoint would she have left her husband there all by himself. She in turn had tried to persuade them to go home to rest and come back in the morning, especially the older women, but nobody did. Although they were nodding off in their chairs, no one would leave the vigil, as if competing to see who could hold out the longest.

She'd left the coffin only to go to the bathroom, to check on her sleeping children, and at one point when the room was so packed that the fans were useless, and what with the smell of cigarette smoke and flowers and the lack of ventilation, she felt her legs weakening and had to go and get some air.

Her godmother had led her out by the arm, alone, refusing the other women's help, and once they were on the patio, the people waiting to go in and say their last goodbyes to Miranda vacated one of the benches so they could sit. Some seemed about to come over and offer assistance, but Señora Nena waved them away with extravagant hand gestures, as if they were pigeons swooping down on a piece of bread.

Estela leaned against the wooden backrest and lifted her face to the tree that cast its shadow over the bench. She gazed at the leaves and, through the gaps in the green, at the sky, the sunlight of the first hours of the morning.

Her godmother scooted to the other end of the bench and lit one of those short, pungent cigarettes she liked. She'd moved so as not to bother Estela with the smoke, but her goddaughter reached out and felt for her hand, looking upward all the while. Señora Nena laced her fingers through hers and there they stayed, hands clasped, in silence. The old woman blew out the smoke and glared fiercely at the people hovering nearby, so that no one even dreamed of approaching with condolences or small talk.

It was no more than ten or fifteen minutes, but it did Estela good to be away from the others for a while, her mind blank, her gaze fixed on the calm, still leaves.

"Shall we go back?" she said when she felt ready.

"Okay, dear. If you want. But wouldn't you rather stay a little longer? I could get you something to drink?"

"No . . . I'm feeling better now."

"Sure, darling?"

"Yes. It's time."

Her godmother stroked her cheek and Estela turned her head, nuzzling the old woman's palm with her nose. It smelled of tobacco and that sickly sweet perfume she always wore.

"Come on, then."

They stood and went inside.

By now the room was full of people. Her godmother put an arm around her shoulders and cleared a path through the crowd; there was a murmur as the widow passed.

In bed, Estela stroked the empty side where Miranda used to sleep. She turned their double pillow around so she could put her face where, for so many nights, her husband had laid his head. It had his smell. Which, that night, was already becoming the memory of his smell.

When a few days had passed since Tamai's summons and he hadn't been called back, Celina began to relax, to take her husband at his word.

He might have sworn on his own life that he had nothing to do with it, but she didn't quite believe him. Deep down she still hadn't decided if she thought he was capable of killing someone. Did she think he wasn't? Or did she just want to think that?

Perhaps Tamai, in his right mind, wouldn't have had the courage, but she knew her husband was a nasty drunk and she could no longer vouch for him. Sometimes he'd leave the house with a knife in his belt. He'd say he was off for a barbecue with the guys, and all evening she'd have her heart in her mouth, fearing the worst until he came home.

A man can be docile enough till alcohol clouds his head and he spots a chance to play the tough guy, as she knew well enough from all those years in her father's bar. More than once she'd seen the meekest of indios pull a knife on a friend over nothing. More than once someone had gotten hurt in those skirmishes, despite her father's quick reflexes when he threw them out into the street at the first sign of trouble, whether or not they were wearing shoes. Her old man wasn't scared of them, though he did end up with a scar on his arm from one of those nights when his patrons crossed the line.

And Tamai wasn't exactly meek. He'd given Pajarito real

thrashings after a few drinks, and when she tried to stop him, he'd turned on her as well. If he had the stomach to beat a little kid as if he were hitting a man his own size, something wasn't right. He hit her, too, but that was by the by: men always wound up hitting their wives in the end. She'd learned that too. After all, hadn't her father taken his belt to her when she told him she was expecting Tamai's child? But as for hitting a defenseless kid, well, that was completely different.

All the same, guilty or innocent, something changed in Tamai after Miranda's death. He became increasingly withdrawn. His character, gloomy in the best of times, grew darker. At home he barely said a word, and he headed off earlier and earlier to meet the guys at the bar. He went from not working much to hardly working at all. He even seemed to have lost interest in tormenting Pajarito.

Some time ago, unobtrusively, so as not to hurt his pride, Celina had begun to take charge of the brickworks. Since Tamai wasn't putting in much effort, she and her eldest son would help him fill customers' orders. At first he got annoyed and hounded them constantly, finding fault with everything they did. But he soon saw the plus side and even started acting like a kind of boss, giving orders and supervising their work.

After the neighbor's death, that stopped as well. He watched them come and go, lugging earth around in the blazing sun, but he didn't even bother to carp at them. So Celina decided to hire a guy to help out.

She thought Tamai would throw a fit when she told him the news, but no. He shrugged and, just to say something, to give a nod to his old self, he dug up a shred of cynicism and retorted, "He can help you out in bed while he's at it."

Now, with the work taken care of and money in his pocket, business having picked up since his wife took over, Tamai's absences grew ever more prolonged. Celina thought there might be another woman, but that was neither here nor there: he no longer mattered to her.

And one night it came, the thing she knew would come sooner or later. And that, truth be told, she'd been wanting to be done with.

The kids had gone to sleep and she was getting ready for bed, hanging up some laundry, when she saw him approaching. Surprised he was home so early, she thought that he'd come to ask for money, that he'd lost it all in a hand of cards and needed more so he could keep playing. Mentally, she prepared to refuse.

However, he pulled a chair from under the table and sat down. He motioned for her to sit down too. Celina was alarmed, always expecting the worst.

Tamai lit a cigarette and gave it to her, then lit another for himself. He was sober.

"I'm leaving," he said.

Celina felt her blood run cold.

"What did you do?" she asked.

He gave her a long look. Tamai's yellow eyes, which only anger brought to life, glinted almost sadly in the darkness.

"Nothing," he said at last.

She let out a breath, slightly ashamed of her question. Ashamed, and also sad, at having lost faith in him years ago.

"I'm sorry . . . it's just . . . ," she stammered.

"Forget it." He cut her off with a wave of his hand.

"And what do you mean . . . leaving?"

"I got in with some guys headed for Mendoza to harvest potatoes. We're taking off in a bit, there's a truck."

"It's cold there," she said, finishing her cigarette and stamping it out with her sandal.

"Apparently so."

"And how long will you stay?"

"I don't know. There's no place for me here anymore."

She nodded. He stood up and went indoors.

Celina followed in silence, not knowing what to say. She watched him pick up a large bag and stuff in some clothes. Then he opened a dresser drawer and removed a shoebox where they kept the papers and cash. He took his documents and some banknotes and showed them to Celina. It wasn't much. She nodded her approval.

"Say bye to the kids for me," he said, and kissed her on the cheek as he walked past.

"Take care, Tamai," she said in a small voice, not turning to see him leave.

There was a time when Pajarito Tamai and Marciano Miranda were friends.

In the streets, empty lots, and roadside ditches around La Cruceña, all the neighborhood kids banded together to form an indistinguishable mass, a single army of children, whatever their surname or provenance. Pajarito, Marciano, and the rest were no more than their first name or the nickname the others gave them; family was just where you went back to, to eat and sleep. At most, family meant being another kid's brother or sister or cousin. But nothing beyond that.

On one block alone there lived some twenty children ages three to twelve . . . and younger ones, too, but the basic requirement for joining in the games was being able to walk; if you could speak or make yourself understood, that was a bonus.

Pajarito's sister, Sonia, led him into the group by the hand. He still couldn't quite walk by himself, but Sonia, not wanting to be holed up at home, dragged him everywhere she went, or gave him piggyback rides, and when she got tired—being little herself—she asked another girl for help and between them they took one arm each, guiding his baby steps.

Soon Pajarito became everyone's pet. The girls made a living doll of him, cradling him in their arms, dressing him up, feeding him imaginary dishes, serving him tea. And for the boys he was the eternal captive tied to the post and the butt of every joke.

That lasted until he turned three and could hold his own against Sonia's horrible girlfriends and the bigger boys and start properly taking part in the games.

That initiation period toughened him up and taught him to look after himself.

Marciano, on the other hand, joined when he was older. Well past his fourth birthday, and able to walk, talk, pee, and poop all by himself.

It wasn't easy for Estela, letting him go off with the neighborhood kids. She was afraid something would happen to him. The others were older and played rough games, they climbed trees, went fishing without asking first or even letting their mothers know. Those women had lots of children and not much time to worry what the bigger ones were up to. For them, it was a relief if they disappeared for a few hours straight. But Miranda put his foot down.

"Stop fussing, Estela, let the boy go and play with the others. Look at him, the poor thing, nose glued to the fence all day long watching the others having fun: he's like a prisoner. They're all tiny, what's going to happen to him?"

"I don't know . . . some of them are little savages."

"Oh, come on, woman . . . Kids are going to be like that. Or do you want him to wind up a mama's boy?"

"What if something happens to him? The other day the kid from the corner shop slashed his leg open on a piece of metal. You should've seen how the poor thing was bleeding. His mom almost had a heart attack when they brought him home."

"C'mon . . . Don't be so dramatic. What about all the knocks and bruises I got as a kid? And I'm still here. It's time he grew up. Or he'll be a damn sissy when school starts."

And it was Miranda who led him by the hand to play with the others.

"Hey, kid, come over here. Yes, you, come here," he called to one of the oldest, who came running.

"Yes, Don Miranda."

"This here's my son, Marciano . . ."

"Like a martian?" the kid laughed.

"And you, what's your name . . ."

"Rubén Otazo . . ."

"He's lying, mister, he's called Cabra, 'cause he looks like a goat," said another kid, giggling, who'd come to see what was going on.

"Shut it, you . . . ," said Cabra.

"Well, Rubén . . . or Cabra. I'm not laughing at your name. We're all called what we're called and it's not something to laugh about. Agreed?"

"Yes, mister. I didn't mean to."

"Right. This here's my son. And he's come to play with you."

"Okay, Don Miranda, leave him with us."

"He's still little and he's not used to other kids."

"Hasn't he got any brothers or sisters?" asked the nosy kid who'd interrupted Cabra, amazed.

"No. He doesn't."

"Weird . . ."

Miranda frowned at the kid.

"Bit of a smart aleck, aren't you? Always got something to say."

The kid laughed and shrugged. He was missing two teeth. He was skinny with jet-black skin, and his hair was cropped close to his head.

"Why'd they cut your hair like that?" Miranda asked. He'd taken a liking to the kid.

"Oh," he said, scratching his head. " 'Cause I got nits. But they're gone now, mister."

"He still can't stop scratching," said Cabra.

"I see. Anyway, I'm leaving my son with you. And I want him back in one piece, you hear?"

"Yes, Don Miranda," Cabra answered quickly, solemnly.

"Go play with the kids, son. Go with these two. They'll take you, okay?"

"Yes, Dad," said Marciano, grinning from ear to ear, and he took Cabra's hand and the three ran off into the wasteland.

Miranda watched until they disappeared in the throng of children, then went home laughing to himself. Estela was waiting with the maté gourd ready.

"Well?" she asked, anxious.

"Well what, woman? Well nothing. He went off as pleased as punch. One thing, though. I think we're going to have to cut his hair."

"Cut his hair? How come?"

He chuckled and shook his head.

"Those kids are crawling with lice."

Estela sipped the maté and said nothing. Lice were easily dealt with. She just prayed nothing bad happened to her little boy.

After his father introduced him to the others, Marciano became part of the gang in no time. Despite growing up all by himself at home, he wasn't shy, plus he had the protection of Cabra and the other boy, who everyone called Gorgojo, or Weevil.

As soon as he got up, he'd gulp down his milk as fast as he could and go running out to play, by which point the others had been in the street for a while. And when he was at home, he never stopped talking about his friends.

With time, Estela grew more relaxed. But she missed her little boy. They'd been so close when he was younger, and since Miranda wasn't one to spend much time at home, her son being there made her feel less lonely. So she began thinking of having a second.

She'd been the only child of a single mother, who upped and left soon after she was born. She was raised by Señora Nena, who'd never had children herself. She'd often wished for a brother or sister. Even now, every so often, she thought it would have been nice. Though maybe she did have a few, somewhere out there. Her mother had been a young woman when she'd left and had probably had other kids.

When she told him her plans, Miranda was on board right away. He'd always wanted more than one child. Although he'd fallen out with his own siblings after a row over the inheritance, and they'd gone off to Buenos Aires and he'd eventually lost track of them, he thought having a big family was important.

It must have been on one of those scorching afternoons, streaks of sweat marbling their dust-covered skins, enjoying a pile of bitter oranges plundered from some orchard, that Marciano and Pajarito became friends. They were the same age and they both had guts: they weren't scared of heights or dogs or bigger boys.

Cabra and Gorgojo, seeing that the babies of the group made a good pair, took them under their wings like a pair of aging gangsters training their successors. The protection of the two older kids brought them closer. Back then there was no jealousy or rancor, far from it.

The only thing they found kind of odd was the ban on going to each other's houses.

One time Estela invited them all in for their milk. It was a whole little party on the patio. Pajarito, of course, was a guest of honor, along with Cabra and Gorgojo. They were all clustered around the table, snatching up alfajor cookies and sponge cake, competing to see who could cram the most into their mouth, when who should ride by on his bicycle but Tamai. He spotted his son in the gaggle of kids, slammed on the brakes, and called to him from the street. He had to shout a couple of times, because with the racket they were making, Pajarito didn't hear. In fact, it was Estela who saw him and went to see what he wanted.

"I'm calling my son, ma'am."

"Which one's your son, Tamai?"

"That one there . . . Pajarito. Pretending he can't hear. Pajarito! I'm calling you, for Christ's sake."

"Leave him be. He'll finish his milk and then I'll send him home."

"No, ma'am. No offense, but I won't have any of my children setting foot in your house, understood?"

"They're kids, Tamai. They've got nothing to do with whatever problems you have with my husband."

"I'm not going to argue with you, ma'am. You can raise your son however you see fit. But I wouldn't have mine in that house even if you paid me. Pajarito! Get out here, that's an order!"

Finally Pajarito noticed he was being called. When he heard his name, he turned to see where the shout was coming from. He looked scared shitless when he saw his old man.

"Get over here! We're leaving."

"Tamai, please . . ."

"And the same goes for your kid. I don't want him in my house, understood?"

Estela nodded.

Pajarito walked past her, burning with shame.

"Get back home now, boy, your mom wants you!"

Once he was through the Mirandas' gate, Pajarito set off for the other end of the block at a run.

"Don't punish him . . . It was my fault . . . I invited them . . . They're only little."

But Tamai had already picked up speed on his bicycle and was disappearing around the corner.

When Estela told her husband what had happened, Miranda slammed his fist down on the table.

"Jesus fucking Christ," he said.

"There's no sense mixing up the kids in grown-up problems," said Estela.

"No. All the same, best if Marciano doesn't go over there either. That loser would do anything to fuck with me."

"I don't think he treats his children right . . . You should have seen how scared the poor thing was when he left . . . like he'd seen the devil."

"Devil is right. The man's a snake. I ought to go over there right now and give him a piece of my mind."

"Leave it, Miranda . . . don't you start."

"Oh, so now you're having a go at me. Tamai comes around here making a stink and suddenly I'm to blame."

"I told you so you'd know, that's all. Not so you'd go over there stirring up trouble. The kids are friends. They don't understand all this grown-up silliness."

"Fine. But Marciano needs to know that he can't go over there."

"I'll talk to him."

From that day on they were banned from setting foot in each other's houses, but not from being friends. What's more, their fathers' feud, the feeling of going behind their backs, strengthened their bond. It was a few years before they, too, would end up at odds.

Now his bones are frozen. And in the earlier memories, he finds refuge. A fairground like this one floats into view, only in broad daylight.

You have to cross the whole town to reach it. He and his friend get on their bikes and pedal over the loose dirt roads of their neighborhood, then the gravel of the streets closer to the center. It's hard going and the bike wheels fling pebbles out to the sides, some of which sting their bare legs. Two or three paved blocks: sweet relief. They let go of the handlebars and fold their arms, showing off. There's no one around. Not a soul in the big square. They stop and lean their bikes against a tree, then run over to a tap.

Pajarito gets there first, turns the tap on, and sticks his mouth under the jet of water. He spits it out with a shriek.

"It's boiling!" he yells.

The other boy hoots with laughter.

They let the water run, Pajarito testing it with his hand. When it's just about drinkable, he puts his lips to the tap again. His cheeks bulge and water gushes from the corners of his mouth, streaming down his neck. The other boy shoves him aside and follows suit. Pajarito falls on his ass in the wet grass, in the muddy puddle that's formed around the tap. He grabs the other boy around the neck, making him splutter and spit out the water. They roll over the blotchy grass and soil, laughing, and end up flat on their backs, struggling for breath.

Refreshed, they return to the bikes in silence. This time they trade and ride each other's. More pedaling in the hellish siesta-hour sun. More gravel, then more dirt roads. The tires hiss over the loose dust, leaving marks as they go, like snakes.

They can't have been more than six or seven, because in third grade they both made new friends and parted ways for good. And in this memory they're still pals.

They'd snuck out during the siesta without permission. They planned it that morning after hearing the ads: "The biggest fun fair in the country," boomed the loudspeaker fixed to the roof of the Renault hatchback. "Better than Italpark!"

As soon as everyone was asleep, they met on the corner with their bikes. It was the farthest they'd ever gone by themselves, but they knew the way, it was pretty straightforward.

And there they were. The town center more and more distant. The houses and streets more and more like where they lived.

"No waaaaay," Marciano exclaimed and slammed on the brakes.

Pajarito, zooming along, got a few yards ahead before braking as well.

"No waaaaay," he echoed and looked back at his friend.

"Yes waaaaay," they both shouted and burst out laughing.

A dog barked in a yard somewhere.

Marciano pedaled slowly to catch the other boy up. They stood side by side in the middle of the road, looking straight ahead. The Ferris wheel was silhouetted perfectly against the blue sky: a giant circle with multicolored edges, easily clearing the roofs of the buildings nearby.

"Come on!" said Pajarito, pressing down hard on the pedals and the chrome handlebars that gleamed in the sun, hunching over to go even faster.

The two were neck and neck and the only sound was their panting and the gears whirring with the speed.

They soon reached the field.

The fair wouldn't open till the evening, and although everything was almost ready, there were still some men at work.

They flung their bikes in the dry ditch and went in. First they walked around the stands. Brightly colored metal kiosks each marked with a different sign: hook-a-duck, ring toss, shooting range, raffle . . . They all had their shutters down, keeping the treasure trove of prizes safe within. Marciano stopped at the last one and elbowed his friend, nodding toward the sign. Kisses 0.50, it said.

Then they went to where the rides had been set up. They walked past the trampoline: it was huge, like three double beds put together, but round, and way taller than they were. And then the caterpillar, the tagada . . .

"One time I went on the tagada and then I puked everywhere," said Pajarito.

The roller coaster, the bumper cars, the teacups. So many rides. Maybe it wasn't Italpark, like the ad claimed, but it was the biggest fair that had ever come to the town, by far.

They stood and watched a guy who was adjusting some screws with a very large wrench. The guy was on a metal structure more than six feet above them. He wore serge overalls and a hat to keep off the sun. A lit cigarette dangled from his mouth as he worked.

"What's that, mister?" asked Pajarito, raising his voice so the man could hear him.

The worker looked down.

"We're closed," he said.

"We just came to have a look," said Pajarito, hands cupped around his mouth to make a megaphone.

The guy kept one hand on the iron pole and with the other, which held the screw, took the cigarette from his lips. He blew out a stream of smoke and looked at them.

"What's that?" Pajarito asked again.

"This?" said the man, knocking on the metal with his wrench.

"This here's the pirate ship." And he pointed to a bulky form concealed under a green tarp.

The boys looked over.

"Want to see?"

He tossed his cigarette and it fell near Marciano's feet.

"Watch it!" Pajarito joked, laughing.

The man began to climb down. Several feet from the ground, he let go and jumped, landing right in front of them.

"Give me a hand, then," he said.

They went over to the green shape and he untied some thick ropes.

"Right, you hold on there. That's the way. Now pull."

The pirate ship was huge, so the guy had to climb onto the tarp and lift it bit by bit. The boys helped from below. Finally, after a lot of maneuvering, the ship was revealed.

"Wooooow," said the two boys in unison.

"Hop up," he invited them from his perch on the edge of the boat. "There are some steps on the side there."

He didn't have to ask twice, and they were up in no time.

The guy was rolling a cigarette. He'd unbuttoned his shirt, and his chest was shining with sweat.

Pajarito and Marciano explored the boat. Really it was just a painted structure with a bunch of seats and safety bars.

"Well? Like it?"

"It's awesome. And how does it work, mister?"

"This fixes in the middle there and it swings from side to side. Might not sound like much, but it can really get going."

The worker lit his cigarette and took out a handkerchief and wiped his reddened neck and chest. He glanced around. A few yards away he saw three of his colleagues putting the finishing touches on the roller coaster, and beyond them another two setting up the swing boats. The rest were taking a break in the trailers at the far end of the field.

He let his gaze fall on the kids. They had their arms slung over the side of the boat, and they were standing on tiptoe, looking down. Their skinny brown legs emerged from their shorts, and their T-shirts had ridden up, revealing a square of each torso, the base of the spine.

"You boys want a Coca-Cola?" he asked.

In third grade, Marciano and Pajarito stopped being friends. Three was a crowd and the third, for them, was Nango, who had moved to the neighborhood with his family from Charata.

In first and second grades, Miranda's and Tamai's little darlings had sat together, causing their teachers constant headaches. The third-grade teacher, warned by her colleagues that the pair were a handful, used the new pupil, Nango, to split them up. The moment they came into the classroom, she declared that the new kid would share a desk with Pajarito, to help him fit in, as she explained when the two friends refused to budge.

Miss María Nieves was unswayable and had no time for their pouting, tears, or needy hugs, those childish ploys that melted other teachers' resolve. She had a tough reputation and the respect of her colleagues: María Nieves was never afraid to show the little terrors that she meant business.

Although Marciano and Pajarito tried to argue, it wasn't long before they gave up: they knew that disobeying the teacher, this teacher, on the first day of school, meant repeating the grade. If you got on the wrong side of María Nieves, you were stuck there for good.

So Marciano picked up his satchel and went where the teacher told him. And Pajarito sat down, staring straight at the board, determined not to say a word to the new kid: if it was help fitting in he wanted, he could find it elsewhere.

That's how they spent the first few days: Pajarito in the front row, ignoring the new kid, Marciano some rows behind, sitting with one of the teacher's pets, and the teacher herself like the cat who got the cream, lording it over her colleagues because she'd neutralized the pair.

They hung out together during breaks, plotting to ambush Nango after school and get revenge. But there was always someone, his sister or mother, waiting to pick him up, so they couldn't put their plans into action.

Then one day, out of weariness or boredom or necessity, Pajarito and Nango struck up a conversation. The new kid lent him a map; he slid it over without being asked, and before María Nieves caught him without the right materials.

At break he told Marciano, and his friend, hurt, said, "Bringing two maps. What a loser!"

Loser or not, he owed him one. Maybe he wasn't so bad after all, and anyway, it wasn't his fault the old harpy had sat them next to each other.

After the map came pencils, an eraser, a protractor . . . Pajarito only ever had half the things he needed, because he was always losing them or leaving them at home.

Even though outside the classroom Pajarito and Marciano were still the dynamic duo, Marciano, from his desk, could see that his friend spent classes whispering away with the new kid just like they used to back in the day.

So he thought he'd better find some friends of his own before he got completely abandoned.

With Marciano busy palling around with other kids, Pajarito felt freer to be Nango's friend and now they could hang out during breaks as well.

Besides, being Nango's friend had a lot going for it: his father was a long-distance bus driver and always brought back toys from

Buenos Aires, amazing, brand-new toys that in their town only the rich kids would have, if anyone; plus he could go and play at Nango's house and have Nango come to his without Tamai getting in the way.

Although you could say the split was mutual, deep down they both bore a grudge. Pajarito, like Marciano, felt rejected by his friend.

Not for nothing were they their fathers' sons, each one a chip off the old block. That minor grudge, as time went by, hardened to stone in each boy's heart. And by the winter holidays, the pair, who'd been inseparable until the summer before, were irreconcilable enemies.

His dad is gone. Marciano doesn't know if that's good or bad. If his dad left because it's still not time for Marciano to leave with the dead man. Or if his dad was scared away by the nearness of his death.

How to describe it? His dad was acting like he didn't know he was dead. First he recognized him as his son, then he seemed kind of distracted, and in the end he treated him like a stranger.

His dad doesn't know he's dead. He went on wandering through that final night, always on the way home, always late, always thinking about the dressing down he'll get from Estela for coming back at that hour.

Although it's been ten years, Elvio Miranda still hasn't made it into the afterlife. He's stranded in those few minutes before the murder; he can't let go of the land of the living. Is he after revenge? Maybe so. But the one person who could avenge him, who swore on his dead body to settle the score, is about to bite the dust.

It's his son Marciano, his firstborn. Ironic, him being the one to find the kid here, bleeding out at the fairground. Elvio Miranda pretends he doesn't get it, pretends he hasn't caught on, because the day he accepts the system, he won't be able to keep one foot in each world, won't be able to carry on making his little getaways.

But what a goddamn shame, it being his own son collapsed here in the mud. He left just now because who knows, if he refuses to do his bit, maybe the kid will be saved. He's not sure how this stuff works. But for him of all people to have to collect him and take him away, that would be too cruel. Although, thinking about it, it's right that it should be him: if he brought him into this world, he ought to take him into the next.

He doesn't know. Better to leave. Better not to find out. He turns away and doesn't look back. If he, who's more from there than here, can't see him, maybe it's because the kid is going to live.

Estela would never forgive him. She'd never forgive him for taking her little boy. Had she forgiven him, even, for dying? Sometimes yes and sometimes no.

At first Estela couldn't afford the luxury of being furious: not with her husband, or with his murderers. After the initial paperwork came figuring out how to keep things going without Miranda, with the brickworks, with the children. Plus the constant visits from Rebolledo, which brought no more than a pale glint of hope when the police car parked outside, then a rush of disappointment when the officer shook his head and said: "Nothing yet."

Nothing yet was the same as nothing forever: the more time went by without any breakthroughs to report, the less likely it was they'd ever find the culprits.

The whole thing would have been much easier if Tamai were the murderer, but Estela always knew he had nothing to do with it. She couldn't explain how, but she knew. Easier because everything would have been sorted out in no time. That said, she was glad it wasn't their neighbor. He had his own wife and kids, his oldest boy was in Marciano's class at school, and it would have been too much sorrow for one neighborhood to bear.

She wanted them to find the murderers so her husband could rest in peace, but also, most of all, so her eldest son could live in peace. She hated seeing him so angry. So silent and with who knew what dark thoughts swirling in his head.

After a few months, when she was starting to feel resigned, came the robbery of the provincial bank. She realized then that the investigation into her husband's murder, which had already stalled, would be put on the back burner for good.

Two or three weeks passed without Rebolledo stopping by. One afternoon he turned up and wouldn't even accept a drink of maté.

"Can't stay long," he said. "This bank robbery business is driving us up the wall. I don't want you to think we've forgotten your husband, but you know how it is. We're not prepared for so many big cases at a time—this bank stuff, there's never been anything like it, not even in Resistencia. I'm telling you, they're no more prepared than we are."

Estela waved her hand, as if saying not to worry.

Rebolledo patted her on the shoulder.

"And how are you holding up, Estela?"

"Fine. Adjusting."

"Good, good. Well; I'll stop by another day for that maté."

And off he went, with his loping gait.

Maybe that was the afternoon when her fury set in. First with the police for not turning up any leads. Then with the murderers. And then with Miranda himself. Because it was his fault that what happened to him had happened. His fault for leading the life he'd led. He'd abandoned them, his own family, and left them to fend for themselves. And it was his fault poor Marciano was going through hell.

The fury lasted a long time. Then Estela shifted back to resignation. There was no point staying angry at a dead man; it's not like he was still doing her harm.

Then she began to light candles for him every day, to speak

to him when she got into bed and the kids were asleep and everything was silent except for the barking of the dogs, to confide her most intimate thoughts to him as she never had when he was alive. It soothed her to think that from wherever he was, Miranda was listening to her. That now, at last, from wherever he was, Miranda was looking out for his family.

That day when he got up, around noon because there was no school, Pajarito's mom told him their neighbor had been killed. His insides froze and right away he thought of Marciano. How unbelievably lucky he was. It was so unfair—he wished *his* father was dead.

By then he and Marciano hated each other so much they'd forgotten they were ever friends.

Pajarito had gotten close with Nango and some boys he recruited at school and around the neighborhood. Marciano had done something similar. His sidekick was called Luján and he was one of Gorgojo's brothers.

Cabra and Gorgojo had gone off for military service and never came back to the neighborhood. Word was they both went to Buenos Aires to work in construction. They left the two boys as friends, worthy successors. But Pajarito and Marciano didn't share the same bond as their mentors. While the older pair were taking on the big city side by side, they'd turned their backs on each other at the first sign of trouble.

Just as they had divided up their class in school, they divided up the neighborhood outside of it: each gang had its patches of wasteland, its streets, and its times for playing foosball, since there was just one table at the grocery store and sharing was the only option. And when they were teenagers, each was the boss of his own corner of the block.

This didn't stop them invading each other's turf from time to time, eager to scrap, to duck and dive and get the fight out of their systems.

In those battles, the kids on each side always left Pajarito and Marciano alone. No one dared lay a finger on the other gang's leader, afraid of a beating from their own commander if he caught them going near his personal enemy.

Both boys had grown into good fighters. They were trained by a single mind—Cabra and Gorgojo, who understood each other as if they were one—and they'd been good pupils. When they clashed, the others dropped their fists and formed a circle to watch, not wanting to miss out on the show. A circle made of two semicircles, of course, because the two sides didn't mix.

It was glorious seeing them fight.

You could say they each became aware of their own body during those tussles: how over time their fists had hardened and their arms became longer and more supple, how their neck veins would swell as blood surged to their pounding hearts, how their stomachs flattened and the bulge in their pants grew larger.

Rubbing, clutching, shoving, and thumping the other body taught them the changes age was bringing to their own. And in some of those skirmishes they saw themselves, doubled, as if in a mirror.

Pajarito finished his milk and got on his bike and went for a ride. Planning, obviously, to go past the Mirandas' house and see what he could see. He took a detour, not wanting to go straight there, not wanting it to look like he cared. First he set off along the road into town. He pedaled for several blocks at full speed, as if he had places to be, things to do. Then he turned and rode back and eventually arrived at the corner where the Mirandas lived.

He braked sharply and got off his bike and started examining the chain. Peering over the wheel at the enemy ground. There was no one in sight. The doors and windows of the house were all closed to the world. Two dogs were sleeping under the awning and the others must have been shut in the kennel.

He stood up and began wheeling his bike slowly, sneaking glances as he walked. Nothing. No one.

"Terrible, isn't it?"

The voice of the old man who lived next door to Miranda made him jump. He was sitting under a tree, on the sidewalk, drinking maté. He'd be there all morning, waiting to say the same thing to everyone he saw. Pajarito went over.

"You hear what happened?" said the man. "Poor old Don Miranda. His poor wife and kids, too, because, after all, he's dead and gone and can't feel a thing, rest his soul."

"I heard he got killed," said Pajarito.

"That's the least of it. They shot him and slit his throat."

Pajarito looked back at the house, this time without pretending not to. Seeing it all silent and deserted, he felt disappointed, like someone who arrives late to the site of an accident, when there's nothing left to see, all traces of the tragedy cleared away.

"And where is everyone?" he asked, nodding toward the house next door.

"The Brazilian lady came, Estela's godmother. Took them all to her place in town. They asked me to feed and water the dogs. Harmless, they are. All well and good for racing, but useless as proper dogs. Word is they'll announce the time of the vigil on the radio."

Pajarito made as if to leave.

"Want to come feed the greyhounds with me?" asked the old man, who seemed not to want the conversation to end.

"No, mister. I've got an errand to run."

"Your bike broken?"

"No. It's fine now. The chain came off, is all. See you, mister."

"So long," said the old man and he went on sitting there, turning his head from side to side like a caburé owl, waiting for another unsuspecting passerby he could draw into conversation.

Pajarito rode past his house quickly, without looking, in case Tamai was about and called him over, and headed to Nango's.

But his friend wasn't there. His sister said he and some other kids had gone to the Imperio to see Miranda's blood, which was apparently still fresh on the sidewalk.

It's the music and the voices, muffled murmurs that suddenly flare into laughter. It's that hum that gets into his head and brings him gradually back. Then he opens his eyes and blinks several times.

Has the sky gotten lower? White as always but now with little stars whose points are too perfect to be real. They look like cut-outs and they are, silver paper stars stuck to a sky that's nothing but a white sheet, pinned up at the corners, sagging in the middle. Like those fat, slow-moving clouds he liked lying down to watch as a boy.

He's stretched out on something that isn't the ground and he feels good, clean and cologned like when he left his house for the fair. His arm slides off his chest and his fingers tangle in the ribbons hanging from the sides of the table beneath him. The murmur of voices continues: now he can make out snatches of words, a prayer verse mixed in with the odd snippet of gossip, and the laughter, everyone's happy, it feels like a party.

He sits up and pulls off the cloth that's covering him. No one takes any notice. His clothes are disheveled and there's still mud on his pants, and bloodstains. But he feels good. Strong. Ready to get on with the night. It was only a scuffle. He walks clumsily at first, bumps into a group of people chatting, and someone puts a glass in his hand. He drinks. The alcohol burns his parched throat. He has to piss and finds somewhere away from the party, leans one arm on a tin kiosk, and lets out a thick, gushing stream. Tucks his shirt in while he's at it, shakes the dry mud off of his pants, and runs his fingers through his damp hair, blades of grass among the tendrils at his neck.

The whole fairground is dark except for that circle of people and music and murmurs he just left. He's not tired. He could use a couple of drinks to clear his head before going home.

He wanders back to the gathering. Someone hands him another glass. He looks at the faces and they seem familiar, though something's not quite right: everyone looks much younger. Neighbors, relatives.

Candles have been lit over by the table he woke up on. He makes his way through the crowd for a closer look. Although she has her back to him, he recognizes the woman standing at one end: it's Señora Nena, his mother's godmother and his own; a slimmer, younger Señora Nena, straighter-backed. He approaches and peers over her shoulder. Her hands are stroking two small feet peeping out of the shroud. And a man he doesn't know, at the other end of the table, is stroking the head of a boy of around ten. His blood runs cold, and even though he understands now, he has to get closer and make sure. He walks around the table and recognizes himself in the boy's sleeping face.

"Make a wish," a woman says from behind him. "Make a wish and tie a knot in the ribbon, and my angel will carry your wish up to God."

Marciano turns and sees his mother's stricken face.

"We have to make the little angel fly!" someone cries.

"It's time, it's time!" they chorus.

"Bring the fireworks! Careful not to burn his wings! Don't cry, Estela, my dearest. If you get his wings wet, he won't make it to heaven, the poor darling."

He and his mother look at each other for a moment, and as

he lifts his hand to stroke her cheek, Miranda appears and slings an arm around her neck. He has a bottle in his hand and shouts:

"Music! Music! My little boy's flying up to heaven!"

Miranda's face in the candlelight looks devilish: his eyes are red and shining, his laugh drunken, false.

Marciano's knees buckle and he falls. Down the black tube again. Sprawled in the mud again. The sky above whiter than white. The same cold in his bones. The same desolate fair. He twists his head and sees his father. Miranda's come back and he's sitting on the ground. With his long nails like a woman's, he's stripping the bark off a branch, and from his pursed lips comes a long, interminable moan.

"Dad, what are you making?"

He says nothing, just carries on with his task. Eventually he answers.

"A cross for my son."

The cumbia's cranked to the max in the new dance hall. Whenever some new place opens in town, it's bursting with people for a few weeks, until the novelty wears off. In the streets around the building, cars are parked nose to tail. Even the rich kids will go slumming out here when there's someplace new to party: sick of always going to the same old club, they come out of curiosity, for a laugh, and because it's easier to hook up with some chinita from the barrios. And in the empty lot nearby, rows of mopeds, maybe a hundred, most with no muffler on the exhaust because these kids like to make themselves heard.

When Pajarito and his friends turn up, the place is heaving. They'd been at Cardozo's till late. Cardozo was the lucky one in the group who lived alone, since his folks had gone off to be caretakers on some gringo's estate up in north Santa Fe. He stayed in town, kept his job at the gas station. When he's not working the night shift, they all hang out at his place.

They grilled some meat, knocked back a case of Quilmes, and did a few lines, getting keyed up for the party.

The new dance hall has gone all out: two levels, three dance floors, and a VIP area on the terrace. Apparently it's run by some guys from Rosario. Nango, who's a radio DJ now, got them all VIP passes.

"And what the hell is a vipp?" Cardozo asked, frowning at the pass he'd been given.

"It means you're important, man, you don't mix with the proles."

"Right. So what am I doing with you?" he said, cracking up.

"Shut your goddamn mouth. Or I'll have that back off you, okay?"

"All right, all right. Cool it, you nutjob."

When they arrived, Nango, who already knew the layout, headed straight for the stairs. Getting up wasn't easy, the place was so crowded that people were dancing even on the concrete steps.

When they finally made it onto the VIP terrace, it was no better.

"Jeez, there's fucking millions of important people," said Cardozo.

Nango ignored him and went to the bar for some champagne. It was the beginning of the month and they all had money to spend.

For a while they stood around in the VIP area, shooting the shit. There was a bit more air there, but the place was dead. The speakers were quiet and the noise came rumbling up from the other floors. No one was dancing. Obviously the VIP area was more for chatting and PDA.

Cardozo and a pal, who'd gone to check out the downstairs, came back saying the other dance floors were jumping. That's where the real party was at. Drunk chicks everywhere, super up for it. Plus the drinks were cheaper.

They convinced the others, who were getting bored, to go back down. Nango wanted to stay because he'd run into some guys from the radio.

"Yeah, leave the journalist to his vipps," said Cardozo, teasing Nango. They were always vying for Pájaro's favor.

They go down and park themselves on the first floor. The foam party's on the ground floor and Cardozo says it's like a mud bath down there, everyone skidding in slime.

They get some beers. Nango's the champagne guy because he loves that rich-kid shit, and they find a space at the bar and settle in.

Marciano is dancing with Yani, a gringa who's shaken off her evangelical parents to come to the dance. Marciano likes dancing and has good rhythm; Yani melts in his arms. Whenever the steps allow it and he gets her in range, he sticks his tongue down her throat. He likes Yani a lot.

Last time, they fucked. Yani had been a virgin and he's proud of being her first. They say women never forget the guy who pops their cherry. Meaning that even if they split up one day, Yani will never forget him. She'll be an old lady somewhere and still she'll remember Marciano Miranda.

Admittedly, they didn't have a great time. She'd burst into tears after and he had to comfort her. Yani's body is whiter than white and her tits and back are covered in moles.

"Did the flies shit on you or what?" he'd said, trying to make her laugh. But she didn't like the joke and cried even harder.

When he gave her a hug to comfort her, he got hard and desperately wanted to screw again. There wasn't a chance in hell of persuading her, so they got dressed and left the room before their time was up.

"That's what you get for doing it with virgins. And evangelical ones too," Luján said when he told him the next day.

But it wasn't just about getting laid; he loved Yani . . . or at least, he had other feelings for her. It wasn't something he'd talk to Luján about. Or to anyone else.

"Who's the gringa dancing with Marciano?" Pajarito asks Cardozo.

"That's Yani Kowalsky. Her dad's Kowalsky from the Highway Authority."

"Aren't they evangelicals?"

"Affirmative. She's in school with my cousin Ileana. You know how my aunt's switched churches."

"Weird that Kowalsky lets her hang out with Miranda."

"He doesn't. Ileana says her father has no idea. Those people only date each other, you know what they're like, religion rammed down their throats twenty-four seven. As if he'd let her near a lowlife like Marciano. But those gringas are way sluttier than girls in La Cruceña, I'm telling you. Big time. They're depressed as hell because of all the God stuff, and when they cut loose, there's no stopping them."

"Repressed, you mean."

"Whatever. And when they let it all out . . . whoop, whoop, it's party time."

"How do you know all this, man? Ever stuck it in holy ground yourself?"

"Sure I have."

Pájaro snorts.

"Listen to yourself, you wouldn't back down if a bulldozer was coming right at you."

"What is this, Pájaro, you saying I'm bullshitting? You don't know jack about the evangelicals I've had."

"Nah, I'm not saying anything. Now get some more beer, man, it's your turn."

"My turn again, you gotta be kidding. Hey, Mono, I'm look-ing at you, you drink like a fish and I've not seen you reaching for your wallet . . . Too busy helping yourself."

"Stop talking crap. Mono just bought some."

"Sure, sure . . . Look at him there, playing the innocent. Staring into space like a dog getting fucked."

Pájaro lights a cigarette and goes on watching the happy couple. It wouldn't be a bad idea to poach Marciano's girl. He's not into gringas himself, plus this one's kind of skinny, but he could take one for the team. He laughs to himself. It'd be beautiful, priceless, just for the look on his face.

He must be nearing the end. He's obviously lost a lot of blood and he's weak, and being weak is making him a pussy. Because here he is, remembering when he and Marciano were friends. Two pipsqueaks, yea high, sneaking out on their bikes to see the fair.

How old was he then? Six or seven, tops. A fair like this one. Or bigger. With more stuff. Like Italpark, people said. Maybe it wasn't even better than this one. It can't have been because that was about fifteen years ago and now everything's way more modern. But memories are like that: you make stuff bigger in your head or you see it with the eyes of a little kid. Two tadpoles they were, yea high.

They'd stayed longer than they'd meant to, and when he got home, Tamai gave him the mother of all thrashings. Apparently they'd been searching for them all over: in the empty lots, by the canal, even on the hill before the old road out of town, where they sometimes went hunting for birds.

That time his mom didn't stick up for him. She was mad as well. She'd have gotten a few smacks in herself but Tamai was too greedy to share, not slowing down until his arm cramped up and the whip handle had blistered his palm.

And what's more, he found the free tickets the guy from the fair had given them, and used them one by one to light all the cigarettes he smoked as the afternoon wound down into dusk.

He made the boy sit with him under the awning, even though

his ass was on fire from the beating and the wicker seat pricked him through his shorts.

"So you liked the fair, then?" he said, the flame reflected in those yellow eyes as he brought the burning paper to his mouth. Then he left the lit remains on the table till they died out and blew away, black wisps that vanished in the air.

After a few days, when they lifted his punishment and he was allowed to leave the house, he heard Marciano hadn't fared any better. Miranda had flogged him within an inch of his life. He didn't burn his tickets, but he gave them to some local kids on the condition they come by later and tell Marciano what a great time they'd had, how much fun it had been.

Two weeks later, when they could play together again, the fair was moving on. They went to the edge of town and watched the trucks drive past, the line of trailers. They thought they saw the man who'd shown them the pirate ship. He waved from the cab of a truck, sitting next to the driver. But they weren't sure it was the same guy. It could have been someone else. Someone like him.

It wouldn't be the first time one stole the other's girl; their hookups had always been fair game. Even before they were really getting any, back when dating was innocent, just kissing and a hand under the clothes.

Often, without knowing it, they'd slept with the same woman. They both liked the married milf type, and on a few occasions one of the pair had been slipping out the back door while the other was climbing in the window. These women weren't passing up the chance to sleep with two boys in one night, perhaps their only husband-free night for a long time.

He had to find out how much Marciano cared about the Kowalsky girl. No point busting his gut for a passing fling.

And it seems this is his lucky night. Because while he's drinking his beer, alone at the bar after Cardozo and the guys have gone off to dance, who should show up but Marciano's brother, Ángel Miranda, the one the kids say is a fag.

And he must be, dressing like that, in trendy, skin-tight clothes. Pájaro likes to wear tight jeans himself, but this kid also goes in for T-shirts and shirts that cling to his body. If he's a fag, he'll be able to tell him what he needs to know. Fags love gossip.

Still, shitty luck for Miranda, having a homo for a brother. If the old man were alive . . .

"Hey, Pájaro . . . got a smoke?"

Pájaro takes the pack from his shirt pocket, shakes one loose, and offers it. Then he reaches for the lighter and holds out the flame. The boy smiles at him. This is going to be easier than he thought.

"You by yourself?"

"Nah. With some friends. They're around somewhere."

"Been a while since I've seen you."

"I guess we hang out in different places."

Ángel signals to the bartenders, but they're so swamped they take no notice.

"What d'you want?" asks Pájaro.

"Oh, nothing. A beer."

"Here, I just got this. We can split it. You can get another one later."

He gets up slightly from his stool to grab a plastic cup from under the bar. He pours.

"Thanks. I'm dying of thirst."

At that moment another stool is vacated. He pulls it over and sits down, then takes a long drink from his cup.

"You here with your brother?"

"No. As if. I'm with my friends from school."

"Oh. You're studying."

"Yep, fifth year at the vocational. I'm finishing soon. I mean, can you honestly see me as a brickmaker?" he says, and bursts out laughing, throwing his head back.

"No . . . not really."

"I don't have a problem with it or anything. Don't get me wrong. It's thanks to bricks my mother was able to raise us. Bricks and wedding dresses." He laughs again. "There you go, the exact two things you need to start a family."

Pájaro looks at him, straight-faced. What the hell is this kid talking about?

"Bricks for building the house. The dress for getting married."

"Right . . ."

"You don't think about that stuff, huh?"

"Nah."

"You're like my brother."

Pájaro doesn't appreciate this comment. He clenches his jaw and takes a slug of beer. Then he refills his cup, Ángel's too.

"Whoa . . . You'll get me drunk."

"But maybe your bro's thinking about that stuff after all, right? Looks like he's got himself a girlfriend."

"Yeah. Yani Kowalsky. Not that he says much to me. But I'd be surprised. Maybe he's thinking about it . . . But if her dad finds out, he'll lose his shit."

"How come?"

"It's pretty obvious. He's a brickmaker and she's Yani Kowalsky. Plus they're evangelicals . . ."

"Maybe they'd have you instead. Since you're studying and all."

Ángel bursts out laughing again.

"Maybe I'm the one who wouldn't have her."

"And why's that?"

The kid looks him straight in the eye. Even under the switching, shifting colors of the strobe lights, Ángel's gaze is expressive. He laughs, but not happily this time.

"I'm not into gringas."

Pájaro turns toward the dance floor, toward the sea of people pressed together, moving to the music. It's so packed that if you stand still, you can dance without doing anything, carried along by collisions with other bodies.

He went too far, saying that to the kid. What did you expect, you idiot, that he'd tell you he's a fag so you could laugh in his face?

He tries to think of something to say, and when he finally looks back, the stool is empty. The kid's cleared out without saying goodbye.

"Cocksucker . . . drinking all my beer and then fucking off," he mutters.

That week Pájaro worked nonstop and didn't even feel like seeing his friends. Luckily there was shitloads to do. Every time he stopped for a smoke and some cold water in the shade, he thought about Marciano's romance and stealing his precious gringa. Then his thoughts turned to Ángel.

The kid had left him hanging. And it was stupid because he had no idea what he'd even been planning to say to him, but he got mad every time he remembered. He must have gone off to pick up some older guys, sponge a few drinks. Fags'll do that when they're young and good-looking, because Ángel's a good-looking kid. Sell their body for a couple of beers. And the worst part is that they like it, they'd do it for free. But when their fifteen minutes are up, they're the ones who pay. Fags spoil faster than normal men, that's what everyone says.

One afternoon, Nango stopped by.

"Let me jump in the shower, I'm sweating like a pig. Get some tereré going, will you?"

His mom and siblings were visiting Sonia, who'd gotten married and had just had her first kid. She and her husband lived in Du Gratty.

When Pájaro came out of the bathroom, the brickyard hand, having seen that the coast was clear, was getting on his bike to go.

"Hey, leaving already?" yelled Pájaro.

"It's just there's some stuff I need to do in town."

"Listen to this joker," said Nango, entertained. "There's some beers he needs to drink in town, is what there is."

"Fine. Go ahead. But I want you here bright and early tomorrow, okay?"

"Come on, Pájaro, when've you ever known me be late?"

"You make the tereré?"

"'Course. Here you go."

"Man, I am wrecked."

"Lots of work?"

"Ugh . . ."

"Saturday tomorrow, though, man. We gotta go out."

"Maybe," he said, taking a sip from the gourd.

"Don't give me that, man. What's the problem—getting old, are we? Hey, Pájaro, you hear Marciano's screwing that gringuita Kowalsky? Apparently it was him who took her v-card."

Pájaro chuckled.

"And how'd you hear about all this, huh? Were you the mattress, is that it? Or the condom?"

"You know how chicks tell each other everything: who they did it with, what it was like, how many times . . . And all the girls come into the radio to request songs and shout-outs and all that crap. They hang out in the booth, brewing their maté . . . Some of them are real sluts, trust me. Anyway, the maté goes around, comes around, and they tell you this stuff. And yesterday one said Yani did it with Marciano Miranda, blah, blah, blah."

"Uh-huh . . . and listen . . . his brother, Ángel, is it true he sucks dick?"

"Fuck knows. That's what people say. He's friends with all the girls. And when a guy's friends with that many chicks, either he's hung like a horse or he's a fag. And I think with him it's more the second than the first."

"If old Miranda were alive . . ."

"The old man would have torn him a new one, and not the way he likes it."

They laughed. Pajarito almost told him they'd had a beer at the dance hall . . . but thought better of it. Nango would happily rat him out to the guys and he'd never hear the end of it. Plus he gave him the beer only because he wanted some intel. And the little fag didn't know shit.

The next day he finished late, dead tired. He had a shower and went to lie down. It was almost ten in the evening when he surfaced. The heat had let up a bit and the house was silent.

He found his mom on the patio, smoking and reading a magazine. He gave her a kiss.

"You get some rest, darling?"

"Yeah." He yawned and stretched. "Kind of. But I need to sleep for like a week."

"I put some pizzas on."

"Where are the kids?"

"At a birthday party."

"Want me to go get some beers?"

"I already went . . . They're in the freezer, nice and cold."

"Want one?"

"Sure. Or did you think I bought them all for you?"

"Drunkard."

Celina laughed and swatted his backside with the magazine when he walked past.

"Hey, show some respect."

The kitchen was an inferno with the oven on, but the smell of baking dough made his mouth water. He sampled the sauce and snitched a few olives.

He went back to the patio with the glasses and beer. He forgot the opener, so he used his teeth.

"What are you doing? Don't be such a savage. You'll end up with no teeth. And then none of the girls will want you."

"How about you? Will you still love me?"

"I'll always love you."

"Even if I have no teeth? Even if I'm ugly?"

"You could never be ugly."

Pájaro gave her a kiss and Celina stroked his neck and buried her fingers in his hair. He shivered.

"Quit it, you're giving me goose bumps with those claws."

He poured two beers and passed one to his mom. They clinked glasses.

Celina had just turned forty and she was still an attractive woman, in good shape. But she hadn't had another man since Tamai left, not even just to pass the time.

"Why don't you hook up with someone else?" Pájaro asked, suddenly.

She laughed.

"Someone else? Like who?"

"You'd have plenty of options."

"I'm too old for all that."

"Bullshit! You're a hottie."

"Says who?"

"My friends . . . I can't, you're my mom. But if you weren't . . ."

They burst out laughing.

"I'll go check the pizzas."

"Yeah, I can smell something burning."

He hadn't been planning on going out, but Celina talked him into it.

"Go on, loosen up. You've been slaving away all week. You deserve to have some fun."

So he went to his room, got changed, and put on some cologne.

"Are you taking the bike?"

"Yeah. I'll go for a ride and maybe catch up with the guys."

"Take care, son. And don't drink too much."

He'd recently bought a Panther 125, and he made the exhaust roar as he rode away.

He was shit-faced last night. That's what he told himself when he woke up the next day with his head split down the middle, and then, after waking up, when he began to remember. After washing the furry beer-and-tobacco aftertaste from his mouth, downing a couple glasses of Uvasal, taking a cold shower, and coming out dripping wet, towel around his waist, to sit under the awning. After drinking the first matés with carqueja his mom brewed him. And then when she, mischievous, giving him that look that's never entirely maternal, or that at some point, he can never tell quite where, stops being maternal and starts being womanly, sipping the dregs of the maté he'd handed back to her, said:

"Big night last night?"

When he found that for the first time the question bugged him, and the way she looked at him, complicit, hungry for stories, for juicy details, as if they weren't mother and son but two friends.

Maybe then, when he tried to think back and tell her, or when he tried to work out why the situation bugged him when it was the same as every other time he'd had a heavy night, maybe then he remembered all of it and told himself: I was shit-faced.

That was when he got up and went to the room and shut the door and lay down on the bed that was still burning. He lit a cigarette in the dark and began to remember everything, or almost everything. The important things.

Again he sees the neck he's nibbling softly as he clutches a handful of silky dark hair, and the bony shoulders his teeth travel down. He sees himself let go of the hair and plant his hand on the grimy bathroom wall. In his palm, the vibrations of the music from the dance hall, making the bricks throb as if they're alive. His other hand undoing his belt, unzipping, pulling down his pants and underwear; the other boy helping with his own, until they both have their pants around their knees. Pájaro licking, biting, sucking the other boy's back, slapping it with his free hand; the other boy guiding, helping, spitting on his palm, and smearing saliva on his asshole, grasping Pájaro's hard-on, and pushing it in; Pájaro dizzy, grabbing the other boy's cock so he doesn't fall into the puddle of piss and vomit on the stall floor, grabbing it and beating off as if it were his own, pushing so hard from behind it's like it really is his dick he's holding, like it's speared straight through the other boy and out the other side. So he jerks it off as if he's doing it to himself.

The music bursting from the walls. Pájaro's hips moving like he's dancing, his tense arm rubbing the cock in time with the movements of his own, buried in the other boy's soft flesh; warm cum filling his hand. Both of them panting, their legs trembling.

Pájaro pulling out, yanking up his pants, and quickly leaving the bathroom, without a backward glance.

In his room, the shutters closed against the torpid summer heat, Pajarito stubbed out one cigarette and immediately lit another. He pulled the damp towel from his waist and lay naked, the sluggish blades of the fan wafting hot air over his body, lightly rippling his pubic hair, the way the north wind rippled the cordgrass around the swimming holes he went to as a boy. On those afternoons, too, he and the guys would strip and run into the water, into the tepid soup of the lake, feeling the mud at the bottom ooze between their toes.

The water was sensuous, velvety and thick, concealing him from the waist down. He stayed still, feeling the gentle nudges of the waves that reached him from his friends splashing and messing around. His dick hardened and his belly felt strangely hollow. He stayed in that brief trance till one of the guys came up behind him and gave him a shove, dunking him under completely. Then he finally rejoined the others, and whatever had happened to him wasn't happening anymore.

When he tired of playing, he got out and lay on the bank, grass prickling his back and buttocks, and remembered a circus performer who once came to town and lay on a bed of nails. It must be a similar feeling: painful at first, but then pretty good, because after a while he didn't notice the spears of grass, and there he was with his eyes half-closed, looking at the sky, the clouds, the white plumes of the pampas grass, the shadow of a snail kite swooping down nearby in search of food, and the sun burning his private parts.

It's painful at first, but in the end it feels good, if not they wouldn't let you, he thought. They like it, because if not. Fucking faggots.

He stretched out a hand and touched his cock, tugged the delicate skin of the shaft, which was hot to the touch; if he pressed ever so slightly with his fingers, he could feel the blood pulsing.

Why the hell did you stick it in, you dumbass, he said to himself. What an idiot, a few drinks and you'll do anything.

He rubbed his face with his hands and slapped himself twice by the ear. It went on ringing.

He had to go out right away and pick up a chick. Get his hands on some pussy and smell it, stick his tongue deep inside, suck out all the juice, and maybe that would get rid of the stench of piss and shit from the dance hall bathroom, maybe that would get rid of the warm-beer taste left over from last night, and the noise of the music that made his head ache.

He's going to get up and he's going to get dressed. He's going to get on the bike and go for a ride. He's going to find Vero or whoever's around. Get a room at Serra's. Undress the girl, whoever she is, throw her down on the bed, fuck her brains out, wait for a bit, and fuck her again and go on fucking and fucking until the foul memory from the night before is obliterated forever.

The sound of boots going in and out of the mud. Thwack, thwack. The man circles the body, stoops slightly for a closer look, straightens up, narrows his yellow eyes. Suspicious, the old fox. He crouches, farts, lights a cigarette.

"Hey. Can you hear me? Wakey-wakey."

The giggle.

"Quit playing dead."

The kick in the ribs.

"That hurts, you bastard."

"Show some respect, you little shit. Your mother's not here to protect you now."

The yank of his hair, the jerk of his head.

"Open your eyes, c'mon."

"What are you doing here, anyway?"

"Nothing. Just came for a look."

"A look at what?"

"A look at how you're dying."

The guffaw.

"I won't give you the satisfaction, Tamai."

"Aah, seems to me you have one foot in the grave already."

"Shut the fuck up."

Another kick.

"Jeez. You never give it a rest, huh?"

"Look who's talking."

"Uh-huh. Come on, get up."

"Leave me alone. And listen, weren't you off in . . . ?"

"Came back, didn't I?"

"When?"

"A while ago."

"Does Mom know?"

"Nah, 'course not . . . But who's to say, maybe I should swing by the place. She'll need cheering up."

That laugh again with the mouth wide open. Is he missing a tooth? Or two . . . Has he been drinking? Definitely.

"Poor Celina. What's she going to do without her special little pup? Maybe an old dog would fill the gap. Old and randy."

"Dog is right."

The boot on his chest. And what's with that boot? The jeans tucked into the rim, a boot embroidered with green and yellow sequins and pheasant feathers like spurs. He must be kidding.

"You come straight from the carnival or something?"

"Eh?"

"Nothing."

Flamboyant or not, it weighs the same. An elephant's foot on his chest.

"Quit it. I can't breathe."

"Uh-oh. Hope I don't have to give you mouth-to-mouth."

"Funny, aren't you?"

"So anyway . . . I've been hearing . . ."

The dirty laugh.

"Turns out you've been batting for the other team, kid."

"What do you want?"

"To have a little talk, that's all. You're my son. You're dying. Thought I'd keep you company."

"I don't want your company."

"Just think, all your mother got for her troubles was a fudge-packer son."

"Wash your mouth out when you say that shit."

"A goddamn fairy! Jesus Christ. And you thought you were such a player . . ."

Three Saturdays he steered clear of the dance hall and anyplace else he might see Ángel Miranda. He didn't even pass the boy's house; if he had to go that way, he took every possible detour, not caring if it made the journey longer.

He hung out with the guys at Cardozo's as usual, and when they went to the dance, he stayed put. He'd spin some story about how he was boning a married woman. A teacher who lived by the old train station, who he'd had a thing with a while back. How he'd chill for a bit and then head to her place. The teacher had a husband who worked as a night watchman at a tow yard.

He didn't want to go home early. At Cardozo's he was alone, and he felt like being alone. He drank a couple of beers and did nothing. Sometimes the CD the guys left in the player finished and he didn't even bother to change it.

By the fourth Saturday, he couldn't take it any longer. He'd go and find him at the dance, he told himself, and he'd smash his face in. Or give him a scare, at least, since the kid had obviously never been in a fight and he didn't want to take advantage. But he'd knock him around a bit, make it nice and clear that what had happened happened only because he was wasted and didn't know what he was doing. Spell it out, plain and simple: he wasn't into fags, and Ángel should leave him alone.

With any luck, Marciano would step up to defend his little

bro and then they could have a real fight, man to man, and he could wrestle all the rage from inside himself.

That night he didn't go with the others either. He waited awhile, then headed to the dance alone. He parked his bike in what space he could find and then walked. It had rained in the afternoon and now it was cooler. A beautiful night, with that new smell in the air you get after a downpour.

He went in and made straight for the bar. Although it wasn't as crowded as when he was last there, it was still sweltering inside, and it stank. He found a stool and ordered a beer and sat peering around to see if Ángel was out on the dance floor. Nope. He tipped the last of the bottle into his glass and went to check out the other floors. Cardozo was on one staircase, with some chick pressed up against the wall. Pájaro slapped his ass as he went by and his friend spun around to yell. He waved and Cardozo laughed and went back to what he was doing. Pájaro tried to get into the VIP area but the guy wouldn't let him through without a pass.

"I'm Nango's buddy," he said, but the bouncer was having none of it. They'd brought in security from out of town, guys who didn't know anyone, to stop people from sneaking in. Same at the bar, all out-of-towners who wouldn't give away any freebies.

He went down and got another beer, avoiding the people he knew: he didn't feel like mingling, he wasn't there to have fun. Near the bathroom he ran into Vero, who was waiting in line. He was about to pretend he hadn't seen her, but she noticed him, said something to the girl behind her, probably asking her to keep her place, and came to say hi.

"Yo, Pájaro," she said, kissing him somewhere near his ear. A moist kiss: a ticket to whatever he wanted. "Long time no see—where've you been?"

He shrugged and offered her some beer.

"Not right now, I'm about to pee my pants," she said, crossing her legs and clutching herself under her tummy.

"Go on. You'll lose your spot."

"But I'll see you later, okay? Don't disappear on me again, I'm by myself tonight. I'll come find you and we'll have that drink."

He nodded and she ran back to her place in the line.

Feeling dazed from the music, he decided to step outside for a bit. There was a low cement wall by the entrance and he sat there to finish his beer. He lit a cigarette and looked up. Even the stars looked brighter, as if they'd just been washed.

"Hey . . . The party's in there . . ."

The sound of Ángel's voice behind him froze his insides. Before he could turn around, the kid hopped over the wall and stood facing him. He had a glass in his hand and lit a cigarette.

"I needed some air. The place is packed."

Pájaro didn't answer, didn't look. Kept his eyes fixed on the ground. If I look at him, he thought, I'll smash his face in—but at the end of the day it's not worth it, it'd be like hitting a woman or a little kid. His heart was pounding.

Keeping a safe distance, Ángel joined him on the wall. He propped one foot on it, and slung his arm over his knee. Ángel didn't look at Pájaro either. Instead he stared straight ahead, into the distance. His gaze got lost somewhere beyond the reach of the streetlamps.

"I came to find you . . . ," said Pájaro, taking a swig of beer to clear his throat.

"And I found you first," said Ángel.

Pájaro laughed, from nerves.

"Seems so . . ."

"You disappeared . . ."

"Kind of."

"Even my brother was missing you."

"Yeah, right."

They went on drinking in silence, lighting more cigarettes. Pájaro was restless.

"I've got the bike," he said. "Want to go for a ride?"

"Okay."

"Really?"

"Yeah. I love bikes."

"I'll go get it. Wait around the corner."

Ángel laughed softly and took a final drag on his cigarette, then flicked it to the ground and finished his drink.

"Sure," he said.

They met on the next block. Ángel climbed onto the motorbike and held on under the seat with both hands. Pájaro cracked the throttle and they rode across town at top speed. He didn't slow down until they hit the road to La Tigra.

The air was cool and the trees by the roadside formed dark shapes, crisp in the moonlight that bathed the fields.

And when Ángel wrapped his arms around his waist, Pájaro felt, at last, the cold inside him begin to fade.

It was Luján who went and told Marciano.

"Saw your little bro the other day."

"So?"

"He had company."

It made Marciano's blood boil when people came to him with stories about his brother. He'd given more than one person a beating for saying Angelito was gay, and just because Luján was his friend didn't mean he could get away with this shit.

"I'd watch my mouth if I were you, Luján . . ."

They were playing pool and he was so pissed off he scraped the felt with his cue.

"Fuck's sake," he said.

"Let me finish. Don't get mad, you've got to hear it. You won't like it any better if it comes from someone else."

"Go on, then, spit it out," he said grimly, picking up the lit cigarette he'd left on the edge of the table.

"I saw him with Tamai, on his motorcycle."

Marciano burst out laughing.

"Good one, Luján . . . What the hell would Angelito be doing with Tamai? You're just making shit up because I'm winning, moron."

"I don't know what they were doing . . . it's none of my business. But I saw them real late the other night. I was filling up at the Shell and I saw them go by on the bike."

"Real late, so you would've been real drunk." Marciano chuckled and shook his head, then leaned forward and balanced on one leg to make the shot. His last ball dropped smoothly into the pocket.

"Don't say I didn't warn you."

"You lose, smartass. The beers are on you."

They went on playing and drinking and Luján didn't bring it up again. Luján knew his friend well and knew he didn't like people talking to him about Ángel, but he'd seen them clear as day: Pájaro and Angelito, on a motorcycle. He wasn't saying they were doing anything wrong, just that it was weird, seriously weird.

Though Marciano didn't quite believe Luján, he was sure he wasn't lying. If he said he'd seen them, he'd seen them. Luján was his buddy and he wouldn't make that shit up.

True, he didn't have much to do with Angelito. They'd never gotten along and it was his mom's fault for spoiling the kid and making him kind of girly. But it would pass. He just needed to meet some chick who blew his tiny mind and bingo, job done. But what could his brother be up to with his worst enemy?

He had to find out because who knew what Pájaro Tamai was plotting. Poisoning Ángel's mind, turning him against Marciano. The last thing he needed was a traitor in the family.

The next day he asked his mom if she knew anything, and Estela saw her chance to lay into him.

"How should I know . . . You boys never tell me what you're up to. You're just like your dad. I'm stuck here at the sewing machine all day long. Ángel never tells me anything. I don't have a clue where he goes or what he does. Besides, he's too old for me to keep tabs on. And now you come to me with this, when you were always going on about me having him tied to my apron strings. When I finally leave him alone, you want to know what he's doing or not doing. I don't get you two. I raised you both, son, and I raised you to be good people . . ."

Marciano rolled his eyes. Why did he get her started?

"If you hadn't always been so mean to your brother, maybe he'd tell you stuff . . . After all, you're the oldest. You should be giving him advice, seeing as the poor thing lost his dad so young. One of the Tamais, did you say? I doubt it . . . Ángel knows we don't get along with that family. What would he be doing with one of them?"

He didn't even bother asking the twins. Those two were always scheming with Ángel, he covered for them and they'd cover for him, he was sure.

He'd have to find out for himself if his brother was friends with Pájaro.

His mom was right: He'd never had much time for his brother. When they were little, because he was jealous, and later because he was frustrated that the kid wasn't like him and his father. Maybe he'd expected too much and that was why they'd gone their separate ways. He'd wanted to bring him up right, he'd felt it was up to him to educate his brother when Miranda died, but instead he'd only managed to scare him off.

In the days that followed, he tried to approach his brother. How hard could it be: after all, Ángel had always wanted to be friends and Marciano was the one who'd pushed him away.

One night after dinner, he suggested a beer in the pool bar.

"Okay. But just one, I'm meeting some friends later."

This answer irked Marciano, but he kept his mouth shut.

"Fine. Just one," he said.

Since his motorcycle was at the mechanic's, they took Ángel's little Zanella. They made the journey in silence.

They looked for an out-of-the-way table: Marciano didn't want Luján or any other pals joining them. He wanted them to talk man to man.

They lit cigarettes and each one drank from his glass. Ángel was chatty by nature, but now he was quiet, as if not wanting to give his brother too easy a time. That's what Marciano thought, that he was getting revenge, but really the kid was lost in thought, in one thought only: Pájaro. Finally he had something that was his alone, something so vast it made everything else fade into the background.

"So . . . what have you been up to?"

"What do you mean?"

"How're things?"

"Oh . . . fine. Why?"

"No reason. Just making conversation . . . Or are we supposed to drink this beer in silence?"

Ángel smiled.

"You were never much of a talker."

"Well, now I feel like having a chat. What's wrong with that?"

"Nothing. It's just . . ." He was going to say they had nothing to talk about, but instead he trailed off.

"And where are you headed?"

"When?"

"Later . . . You said you couldn't stick around."

"Oh . . . To see some friends. We're just gonna chill for a bit."

"What friends?"

"No one you know. Kids from school."

"You wouldn't happen to have a girlfriend . . ."

Ángel laughed.

"Nah . . ."

"Oh, come on, there must be someone. You're not ugly."

"How about you?"

"What?"

"With Yani. How's that going?"

Marciano shrugged and topped off their glasses. He didn't like talking about himself.

"Are you in love?"

"Don't talk shit, Ángel."

"There's nothing wrong with it."

"How about you?"

"I am, yeah."

"Who with?"

"Aha, ask no questions and I'll tell you no lies."

Marciano's patience was wearing thin. They'd almost finished the beer and he still hadn't found out anything concrete. Why couldn't they talk about bikes or basketball like other guys?

"So, besides the kids from school . . . you got any other new friends?"

Ángel sensed a warning light flash on.

"No . . . ," he said. "But why do you care so much all of a sudden?"

"I'm your big brother. If our dad was still alive . . ."

"Our dad's dead. I don't even remember what he was like."

"Don't be an idiot."

"If he didn't think about us, why should I think about him?"

"You'd better shut up now, Ángel."

"Yeah. I'd better be going."

He stood up and drained his glass.

"There you go. Now we've finished the damn beer."

Through the window Marciano saw him get on the Zanella and back into the road. Fucking kid. Walking out on him like that. He was obviously hiding something.

He got home early, not in the mood to stay out drinking with the guys. When he went to bed, Ángel still wasn't back. He lay there, unable to sleep. Fuming.

In the early hours he heard his brother's little moped pull into the yard. And soon after, the roar of a Panther 125 that died not far off, a block or so away by the sound of it: on the very corner where his enemy lived.

After that night, he kept trying to approach Ángel but the kid wouldn't give an inch, as if he'd already guessed what Marciano was up to.

If he couldn't find out what was going on with his brother, then he'd find out what was going on with Pájaro Tamai. One evening he borrowed Luján's car and kept watch outside Pájaro's place. After dinner he saw him set off on the motorcycle, and followed a safe distance behind. Pájaro zoomed across town. By the eucalyptus grove on the outskirts, he slowed and paused a moment on the concrete lot by the truck stop. Someone got on the back. He returned to the road. By the light of the streetlamp, he saw that the passenger was Ángel. Pájaro sped up again and pulled onto the highway.

Although he'd seen enough, Marciano resolved to see it through till the bitter end. If this was the night of truth, he had to stick it out.

He followed the bike, which slipped from view now and then in front of a truck or another car. Five or so miles out of town he saw them turn off and park at a seedy motel by the roadside.

The boot embroidered with sequins and pheasant feathers soars through the air. The sky has turned from white to blue. But really blue, like in postcards. The boot rotates and glints in the light and on one spin becomes a snake that's spinning as well, rippling through the luminous day, showing now its green back and now its white belly as it turns. Is it dead? He thinks he can hear the creature hissing as it flutters on and on and never lands. He runs after it, like a boy chasing the tail of a kite, he runs through the grass around the lake, clutching his side so his guts don't fall out. He wants to see where it lands, whether it's alive. That's when he hears the sound of the water. Tamai's arm strokes in the lake, his playful splashing, and the invitation:

"Over here! Come on in, the water's lovely . . ."

But he keeps his eyes on the snake as it begins to sink lower and falls into the fields. He runs faster toward it. Thinks about picking it up and lobbing it at Tamai, making the bastard jump, laughing a little.

"Think fast!"

And when he finally gets there, instead of the creature he sees an accordion lying in the grass, splayed open, as if it, too, were trying to escape him. The ivory keys gleam in the sun and when he stoops slightly to pick it up, dizziness takes hold and he collapses into the weeds.

He blinks. The blue sky. And a biguá cormorant soars into

the postcard, flying through the air. Flying and screeching, "Biguáaa, biguáaa," and the screeching of the bird mixes with the screeching of the accordion, gua-gua-guaguaguaguaguaaa.

He uses his elbow to prop himself up.

Tamai, butt-naked, standing on one leg like a heron, is playing the instrument, holding it partly in the air and partly on his raised thigh, moving his shoulders and head to the rhythm of a chamamé. Water is dripping from his hair and he's smiling.

"Didn't know you played," Pájaro says loudly, to be heard over the music.

"There's plenty you don't know. Tamai's a secretive beast," his father says with a wink. Then he raises his head, opens his mouth, and out comes the sapucai shriek from somewhere deep inside him.

"You look like a stud from a telenovela," Ángel said, giggling.

Marciano in the mirror made as if to smack him and the boy laughed again, lay back on the pillow, and started reading the magazine he'd been using to fan himself.

Since seeing him at the motel, Marciano couldn't even look him in the face without the rage rushing back, without the overwhelming desire to beat him to a pulp. He barely spoke to him now, although, to be honest, that wasn't much of a change from how things normally were between them.

He buckled his belt, put on a little cologne, grabbed his jacket, and left the room without saying goodbye.

Ángel put the magazine down and lit a cigarette. That night Pájaro was going out with the guys. He didn't feel like doing anything, so he was staying in to watch TV. Although Marciano had stopped asking questions, he was sure he knew something. He'd warned Pájaro, so his brother wouldn't catch him by surprise.

Marciano gave his mom a kiss. Once out the door, he patted the inside pocket of his jacket: the knife was there, he could feel the ice of the blade. It had belonged to his grandfather, and his grandfather had passed it down to his father, though Miranda had kept it more as a family heirloom; he'd never used it. If he'd had it that night, Marciano always thought, maybe things would have been different.

When he went to his first dances, at fourteen or fifteen, he began carrying it with him. He'd never used it, either, just taken it out sometimes to impress the guys, but he felt safe having it there. He knew how to use it, and if he ever had to, he'd be ready. Luján and another of his friends always went around armed. One time they'd offered him a pistol, but he didn't want it.

"Guns are the devil's work," he'd said, and they doubled over laughing. Firearms weren't his thing.

In his room, Pájaro got dressed as well and put on some cologne. They were meeting at Cardozo's first for some pre-drinking and then they'd kick the night off at the fair. After that, they'd most likely head to the dance hall. It'd been ages since he'd been out with the guys.

"Looking gorgeous, darling," said Celina.

Pájaro laughed and winked at her.

"One of these days I'll end up with no son."

"I'll never leave you."

They hugged.

"Take care, sweetheart."

He got on his bike and rode off.

They were at Cardozo's past midnight. He left his bike there and they all piled into Nango's car. As well as the regulars, Josecito had come with a couple of friends. Pájaro didn't know them, but they seemed pretty cool. Josecito was always showing up with new friends in tow; no one had a clue where he found them, and something told them it was best not to ask.

When they got there, the fair was packed. Everyone chasing the hot new thing as usual.

"By next Friday it'll be dead, trust me. People get bored quick around here," said Nango, who was always grumbling about the ways of the town.

"Here we go, lecture time," said Cardozo. "Give it a rest and let's have some fun, man. Whoa, check out the roller coaster!"

The fair looked great and there were various rides, all lit up and with their own music, and lines of people waiting for each one. It was a beautiful night.

They walked around for a while, had some beers. Tried their hand at the games, but they were all out of luck and skill.

"They make it so no one can win," Nango complained, after failing to get the rings on the hooks for the grand prize: a grubby stuffed animal that seemed destined to stay there forever, aging and fading on its stand.

"Quit whining," said Cardozo. "Or does the poor baby want a teddy bear to take to bed tonight? These games are for pussies, man. Let's see if we can get on a ride."

When they were off the Ferris wheel, Cardozo and Pajarito found the others and made for the cantina. By then, the families and old folks were leaving and only the kids were still around. The beer was cheap, so they were happy to stay there partying before hitting the club or the dance hall.

There were some wooden boards set up on trestles, and massive freezers that kept the beer at that magic temperature: you took a swig and you could chew it between your teeth it was so cold. There were some tables and chairs, too, but no one was using them. The guys were in small groups, drinking standing up.

Pájaro and his friends did the same. Chatting and drinking, cracking up at the stories Josecito's new friends were telling. Entertained and already buzzing from the beer, they paid no attention to what was going on around them.

He would've liked the final scene, the one that flashes before his eyes when they're about to close forever, to be where he and Ángel speed out of town on the bike, in the middle of the night, the engine at full throttle. As soon as they leave behind the trees along the traffic circle, the pale light of the last pool bar, and the line of trucks parked opposite the tire shop, Ángel presses his chest to his back and wraps his arms around his waist, and he feels his chin on his shoulder, little puffs of warm breath at his ear. A scene that's been the same so many times these past months, yet at the same time is always different, always new.

If he could choose, he'd choose the two of them on the bike again. The hot wind in his face, the asphalt shining in the clear night. The feeling that they were masters of their destiny.

But that's not the scene that comes. Instead of Ángel's chest against his back, it's Marciano's chest against his shoulder. Another scene that's been repeated again and again over the years, with slight variations. Sometimes it's his chest against Marciano's shoulder. What doesn't change is that this is the signal they're waiting for to fight.

"Don't fucking push me, okay?"

It doesn't matter which of them says it.

One boy's shoulder touches the other boy's torso, the bodies spring apart, and they step back, plant their feet firmly on the ground, standing astride.

"Who d'you think you're pushing, huh? Huh?"

Chins slightly raised. Eyes locking on eyes.

The rest hardly matters: an afternoon of scalding sun, a cloudy night, the middle of a dance hall, the soccer field in the pink evening light, some street in the center of town.

Meanwhile, the music is always the same: the panting, the sound of fists, the cracking of knuckles before they land the first blow, the hiss of saliva, the occasional groan when a jab lands right in the liver, and the guys egging them on, always slightly hushed so as not to break the spell, and now and then a rapturous cry because their fight is beautiful to see.

Their choreography developed over time, from raw ability to refined skill. Changing along with their bodies. That first contact of shoulder and chest made the transformations clear: one day the shoulder, instead of hitting a bony torso, sank into a swollen pec; the next it met solid muscle, the button of the nipple stiffening at the touch. After the opening move of planting the feet, their T-shirts would come off, the gaze broken for an instant as the fabric whipped past; as if they'd waved magic wands, sparks fly as each studies the other's body, so similar to his own. As the years went by, where once there'd been only teenage skin and bone, now a line of black fuzz emerged, rising from the waist of their jeans to above the navel, branching softly over the chest, forming a shadow. One day their arms stopped growing longer and began growing thicker. Their pants stopped flapping loose from hips to ankles and instead clung to thighs, ass, and crotch. One day they each came face-to-face with a man.

In this scene they're about to fight, but he can't tell who's going to win. Sometimes they both wound up in the dust and their friends had to drag them home. If he can't pick the final scene, he thinks, at least let it be one where he comes out on top.

Fucking tragic to go to his grave with Marciano Miranda kicking his ass.

They're about to fight, but nothing happens. He doesn't know why, but nothing happens. Instead of lunging at him for the millionth time, Pájaro lifts his head and looks at the sky: blue, without a cloud.

Pájaro felt, first, the hand on his shoulder, then when he turned around, the punch in the jaw. He staggered back and the beer bottle slipped from his hand. The guys held him upright. He shook his head to clear it and saw Marciano Miranda standing in front of him, waiting for him to recover. He wanted Pájaro and everyone around him to hear what he had to say before he started up again. And he wanted to give him the chance to defend himself, to make it a fight, a proper duel.

Josecito's friends were ready to jump on the others right away, but Cardozo stopped them.

"This is between them. We'll stay out of it for now," he told them, so firmly they fell in line. Luján and Miranda's lot were waiting, too, squaring up behind him.

"So you're fucking my brother, you fucking fag."

And it all began as a fistfight, the bodies knowing each other at first touch. The smell of the other's blood back on their knuckles; the enemy's smell, fresh and so like their own.

It was Cardozo who saw the flash of silver appear in Marciano Miranda's hand. It was he who, wasting no time, placed his own knife in the hand of Pájaro Tamai. Pájaro stared at him blankly, stunned from the blows. His instinct didn't have to think twice, however. The blades were hungry for enemy flesh.

That's how it began and then came the gunshots, the scrambling, the shouting, and everyone scattered.

The two of them were left sprawled in the mud, a few yards apart. Eyes wide open and fixed on the sky. Everything white. Everything red. Everything white.

The police car pulls up slowly and stops.

Rebolledo and Mamani get out, one on each side, and then, as if they'd rehearsed it, each adjusts his belt under his belly before beginning to walk.

They were here earlier with the ambulance that took the bodies away, and they've come back, now, for a final look.

The fairground is completely empty. The workers are inside their trailers. Unlikely any of them are getting much sleep.

The two officers make their way over the grass, which is ragged like the coat of the old pony tethered between the tin kiosks. Do ponies sleep standing up, like horses?

They return to where Marciano Miranda and Pájaro Tamai fell and died, as quickly as they'd lived.

In the white dawn light, tawny patches of dirt and blood.

Rebolledo lights a cigarette and sighs. He feels defeated.

"How long since we last went fishing?" he asks, clearing his throat and spitting to one side.

"Well, with the summer being so dry . . . ," says his colleague, shaking his head.

"We'll have to go someplace else, where there's water."

"It'd mean going pretty far."

"Even so. It's not like we're needed much around here."

Mamani nods.

Rebolledo casts his eye over the scene one last time. The kids' bodies are gone now, but it's like he can see them.

"What a fucking waste," he says, and crushes his cigarette under his heel.

Selva Almada was born in Entre Ríos, Argentina, in 1973. She is considered one of the most potent and promising literary voices in Argentina and Latin America and one of the region's most influential feminist intellectuals. She has been a finalist for the Rodolfo Walsh and Tigre Juan prizes, and she is the recipient of the First Book Award from the Edinburgh International Book Festival for *The Wind That Lays Waste*. Her work has been translated into French, Italian, Portuguese, German, Dutch, Swedish, and Turkish.

Annie McDermott is a literary translator working from Spanish and Portuguese. Her published and forthcoming translations include *Dead Girls* by Selva Almada, *Empty Words* and *The Luminous Novel* by Mario Levrero, *Loop* by Brenda Lozano, *Wars of the Interior* by Joseph Zárate, and *Feebleminded* by Ariana Harwicz (a co-translation with Carolina Orloff). She reviews books for the *Times Literary Supplement* and is currently based in Hastings, UK.

The text of *Brickmakers* is set in Adobe Caslon Pro.
Book design by Rachel Holscher.
Composition by Bookmobile Design and Digital
Publisher Services, Minneapolis, Minnesota.
Manufactured by McNaughton & Gunn on acid-free,
100 percent postconsumer wastepaper.